WITHDRAWN

BLUECROWNE

BLUECROWNE

A GREENGLASS HOUSE STORY

BY

KATE MILFORD

WITH ILLUSTRATIONS BY

NICOLE WONG

CLARION BOOKS

HOUGHTON MIFFLIN HARCOURT   BOSTON   NEW YORK

Clarion Books

3 Park Avenue, New York, New York 10016

Copyright © 2018 by Kate Milford

Illustrations copyright © 2018 by Nicole Wong

Clarion Books is an imprint of Houghton Mifflin Harcourt Publishing Company.

hmhco.com

The text was set in Bulmer MT.

Map copyright © 2018 by Kate Milford

Design by Sharismar Rodriguez

Library of Congress Cataloging-in-Publication Data
Names: Milford, Kate, author. | Wong, Nicole (Nicole E.), illustrator.
Title: Bluecrowne : a Greenglass House story / Kate Milford ; with illustrations by Nicole Wong.
Description: Boston ; New York : Clarion Books, Houghton Mifflin Harcourt, [2018] |
Series: Greenglass house | Summary: In 1810, Lucy Bluecrowne, twelve, is bored living ashore with her stepmother and half brother until two nefarious strangers identify her little brother as the pyrotechnical prodigy they need for their evil plan.
Identifiers: LCCN 2018006963 | ISBN 9781328466884 (hardback)
Subjects: | CYAC: Brothers and sisters—Fiction. | Stepmothers—Fiction. |
Robbers and outlaws—Fiction. | Fireworks—Fiction. | Chinese Americans—Fiction. |
Supernatural—Fiction. | BISAC: JUVENILE FICTION / Action & Adventure / General. |
JUVENILE FICTION / Fantasy & Magic. | JUVENILE FICTION / Family / Siblings.
JUVENILE FICTION / Fairy Tales & Folklore / General.
Classification: LCC PZ7.M594845 Blu 2018 | DDC [Fic]—dc23
LC record available at https://lccn.loc.gov/2018006963

Printed in the United States of America
DOC 10 9 8 7 6 5 4 3 2 1
4500725522

For Nathan and Griffin and Tess,
with love.

CONTENTS

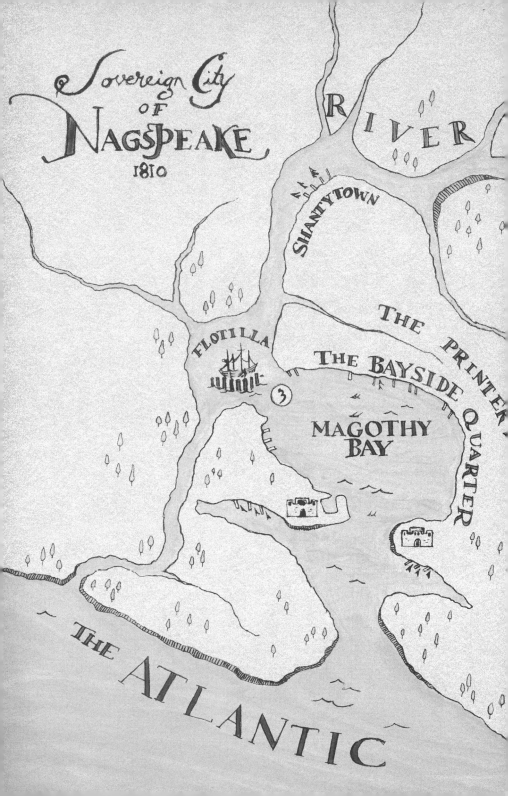

SKIDWRACK

④ ② THE QUAYSIDE HARBORS

① THE HILLTOP

⑤

HIC ABUNDANT SEPIAE →

THE SLOPE

QUARTER

1 *The Bluecrowne Family Home*
2 *The Quenching Press*
3 *Flotilla*
4 *Jonas Forgeron's Workshop*
5 *The House Across the River*

NOT TO BE USED FOR NAVIGATION

ONE

THE PEDDLERS ON THE ROAD

Sovereign City of Nagspeake, September 1810

FOULK Trigemine hiked into both Nagspeake and the year 1810 at the same time. There were different ways of approaching the shift from where and when Trigemine had last been, but when neither the need for hurry nor the making of some sort of fancy impression was a factor, he liked to do it this way: walking easily and leisurely from then to now just as you'd walk from here to there, so that the passage of time took on the feel of a hike along a gusty road, the years passing on all sides like buffeting leaves in a hard wind. As Trigemine walked, the valleys of Virginia slipped away along with the year 1865 in a rush of blue wool and gray cotton, acrid smoke and swirling fuchsia-colored redbud blossoms. In their place rose this high, dusty road lined by blue-needled pines, silver-white birches wearing the flame colors of autumn, and misshapen iron lampposts that stood at odd angles like trees warped by decades of raw winds. From somewhere below the winding ridge road, the scent of brackish water rose to mingle with the odors of turning leaves and warm metal.

There were different ways of approaching Nagspeake, too, but here, at the northern limits of the city, no one would remark Trigemine's arrival. He had been told it was a bizarre thing to behold, witnessing a roamer emerging in time in this manner—that it looked a bit like ice blooming, crystalline, across the surface of water, only worlds faster and with a much stranger geometry. The alternative was to simply and inexplicably *appear*, which could be just as jarring. Up here, on this lonely, forgotten way, no one would see. Except, of course, the man Trigemine was meeting.

The rushing of time subsided and was replaced by applause. "Now that," said a delighted voice from the other side of the road, "that was *something*."

Trigemine turned toward the voice, swept his tall silk hat from his head, and made a bow. "We aim to please at all times."

The stranger hopped down from the seat of a peddler's wagon. The eaves of the wagon were hung with elaborately cut decorations that hinted at flowers and flowing plant shoots, but revealed themselves on second glance to be a filigree of rockets and starbursts, falling stars, and other exploding things. From the back of the wagon a stained-glass rendering of a spinning catherine wheel projected, and on the side the gilded letters that spelled I. BLISTER, PROP glittered even in the shadows of the trees. A piebald pony hitched to the front cropped the weeds that grew along the road.

I. Blister, Prop, strode up to Trigemine with one hand outstretched. He was on the smallish, compact side, with close-shorn salt-and-pepper hair and fingers stained with ash. An oversize velvet coat hung from his shoulders, and a pair of silver scissors-glasses dangled from a chain around his neck. "Good to meet you at last, Foulk. I may call you Foulk, mayn't I? I am Ignis Blister, Founding Member of the Confraternity of Yankee Peddlers and Grandmaster of the Worshipful Company of Firesmiths and Candescents, fourth in precedence among the Chapmen's Guilds." His cheerful voice took on just a little hint of smugness as he finished his recitation.

Trigemine waited out the introduction and worked at ignoring the touch of vainglory in Blister's tone. Ordinarily, if he'd come across a hawker who'd put on such airs while speaking to him, Trigemine would've done something about it. But Ignis Blister was hardly a common merchant on a high horse. Trigemine knew enough about Blister to be wary of him, but even if he hadn't, no mere peddler would've been summoned to help with this task. Morvengarde did not deal with mere peddlers.

And Trigemine was no ordinary peddler himself. "Pleasure," he replied. "Foulk Trigemine, as you know. Victualer and Sutler-at-Large, without precedence or precedent." The two men sized each other up as they shook hands.

"You've come from Morvengarde?" Blister asked. The smugness was gone now, and there was a false note in its place, an oh-so-slightly forced casualness. Talking about the head of the Deacon and Morvengarde Company did that to you, no matter how big a bug you thought you were.

Trigemine found himself liking Blister better. "Sure did."

"And you are the custodian of the famous kairos mechanism."
Blister eyed him, obviously after a glimpse of the item in question.

Trigemine reached into his vest pocket and took the mechanism out: a round double-sided gadget the size of a pocket watch. He held it up, touched a button on the rim, and saw Blister's eyes grow fascinated as six concentric circles unfolded, each rotating on a separate delicate arm. "There it is." *Look down your nose at me now, you pompous devil,* he added mentally. "Which reminds me." A little green pincushion hung on the watch fob beside the device. Trigemine plucked an engraved stickpin from it and held it out.

Blister took the pin and eyed it with interest. "Must I wear it somewhere particular?"

"Anyplace is fine so long as you keep it on your person."

The peddler ran his fingers over the engravings. "It's lovely." He threaded it through the fabric of his lapel. "There. How does it work, precisely?"

"Precisely?" Trigemine snorted. "There's nothing precise about walking through time. Let's just say, so long as you wear the pin, I can use the mechanism to carry you out of the here-and-now and into the there-and-then."

"Nothing precise? Really? I gathered it required incredible exactitude. Meticulous computations and so forth."

"Oh, yes. It requires a world of reckonings, and *meticulous* barely hints at how painstaking I've got to be about them in order to be tolerably accurate in my walking. But it's all to pin down something that, at its heart, resists precision." Trigemine folded the concentric rings back up and closed the device. He turned it over and showed Blister the circular slide rule on the back: an ivory spiral engraved with numbers and symbols. A thin bit of golden mica isinglass overlaid one triangular section like a translucent pie slice. He gave the winder pin on the side a twist and the numbers swirled inward.

"In a nutshell, the mechanism calculates the point at which the passage of time—*chronos*—intersects with *kairos,* the ideal moment for accomplishing a thing. And, of course, the mechanism manages the walking-through-time-and-space bit, as well."

Blister lifted his scissors-glasses to his eyes and peered at the slide rule. "That sounds simple enough."

"Well, it isn't, for three reasons." Trigemine held up his index finger. "One: Time is relative. We call its progression *chronos,* but it isn't *chronological*. It doesn't actually move in a straight line from past to future, so it's not a matter of merely picking a point in time and going there. Two: There isn't a *single* future. There are an infinite number of futures, and an infinite number of pasts as well. So, again, you can't just choose a moment and hop to it, because it's exceedingly difficult to know which future or past you're hopping to. Three: Time is uncertain, and so are the reckonings needed to manipulate it. No matter how careful you are in your workings, there isn't only one right answer to any step involved. I beg your pardon—there are *four* reasons. Because four: By *doing the calculations* you modify every probability in every future or past open to you."

Blister's eyes goggled. "Obviously I understand that using the mechanism—actually walking through time and taking action there—has an effect. Rather the point, isn't it? But simply *working out the mathematics* makes a change? Before one even . . . well, *does* anything?"

"*You* do those calculations and then tell me you haven't done anything," Trigemine muttered. "Yes, the mathematics have an effect. And even before they alter reality, the calculations have their own uncertainty. Imagine I ask you to pin down a moth, but you can see only one wing clearly at any time. You pin that wing, and the other goes fluttering off by itself."

"I imagine I should just try to pin its body."

"It doesn't have a body. There are only those two wings, and you can have only one pin. Doing advanced chronometrical trigonometry is like catching that moth, where the moth is a collection of shifting probabilities, and the pin is a wildly complicated set of equations." He glanced at the reddening sky peeking through the trees. "Shall we head into town?"

Blister waved a welcoming arm toward the wagon. "By all means."

Trigemine climbed up onto the box and stepped awkwardly over a banjo that sat on the seat. He eyed the instrument warily. "What is that thing?"

"It's a *banjo!*" Blister said as he climbed up. He lifted it onto his lap and blissfully twanged a string.

"Yes, I *know* what a banjo is." Trigemine's head twitched as together Blister and the banjo proceeded to create a series of fairly awful noises that did not remotely resemble music. "Is it coming with us?"

"Well, you don't think I brought it with me just to leave it by the side of the road, do you?"

"A man can dream," Trigemine said under his breath.

Blister ignored him, plucking delightedly at the strings. "A fellow's got to practice if he plans to get any better at anything in this world."

The sutler sighed. Getting piqued at Blister over bad music hardly seemed wise. From what Trigemine had gleaned, this cheerful and pompous merchant was also a lunatic who was famous in his circle for being able to blow things up with whatever was lying around—a bit of dust, a single iron nail, a dandelion puff. And that was before he began calling upon any of the truly unique skills that *really* made him a legend. Trigemine leaned back against the seat and pressed a finger between his eyes.

After another moment of cringe-inducing noises, Blister put the banjo down and picked up the reins. "All right. Off we go. By the by, might I know what our adventure's going to be?"

"We're after a conflagrationeer," Trigemine replied as the patched little pony shambled into motion.

For the first time, Blister's sunny demeanor faded. "What's that, again?"

"There's a customer who's ordered up a conflagrationeer from Morvengarde. We're here to find one. And while you find your man, I may be able to pick up an item Mr. Morvengarde would very much like to have as well. This looks to be an ideal time and place to find its keeper."

"Why on earth didn't Morvengarde just call upon me if he

wanted a conflagrationeer's services?" Blister demanded. "Why bother finding another? What does the customer require? Infernal devices? Uncanny fire? A bloody *comet?*"

"This isn't a contract you want," Trigemine said darkly. "I believe the work is a bit more long-term than a . . . a *chapman* of your stature'd care for. I gather it's not so much about wanting a conflagrationeer's services as about wanting the creature itself." Blister scowled at being called a creature, but said nothing. "Less like a contract, I think, and more like a leash."

The peddler's mouth made an exaggerated O. "I see. Someone wants a *pet* conflagrationeer."

"Yes."

"And this is the time and place for gathering one?"

"According to my reckonings, yes."

"So then I'm here to identify the individual in question."

"You are. And, if you can manage it, to recruit him. The fellow we're seeking may be entirely unaware of the roaming world. He may not know his capabilities, or that there's such a thing as conflagrationeering at all. Hopefully you can persuade him to embrace it as his calling and to join us voluntarily. I'd rather we didn't have to behave like a press gang."

"I see," Blister repeated, staring down the road with sharpened eyes. "Still, I haven't run across another conflagrationeer in many, many years. Nor have I heard tell of any. It isn't just a matter of being good at fireworks, you understand."

"I had gathered as much, yes."

"You want an *artificier,* the sort that's neither born nor made.

Anyone can teach himself how to kindle flame and manipulate it. Anyone can touch a match to something flammable and set it ablaze. Anyone with a jot of talent and a bit of will can learn to work with black powder. But a conflagrationeer is not *anyone.*" Blister shook his head. "The archaic term for a conflagrationeer is a *salamander*—a thing born of flame."

Trigemine nodded along, wondering how Blister could simultaneously believe that he was both smart enough to do the phenomenally complicated mathematics of time and space and also stupid enough to have come in search of a conflagrationeer without knowing exactly what a conflagrationeer *was.*

"It's not an entirely false comparison," Blister said in a tone that told Trigemine the other man had noticed his lack of attention.

"I know all this," Trigemine replied patiently. "Of *course* I know all this. But the mechanism has never yet given me false results. This is where and when we need to be in order to find the one we're after."

Blister sniffed. "I believe you." The wagon left the shade of the trees, and the pony clopped along a stretch of road that ran beside a steep decline. Far below, the city spread out on the banks of a sheltered bay. Dozens, scores of ships crowded the water. "I suppose with all the comings and goings in this city, it's the one place I shouldn't be surprised to . . . well, to be surprised. And to meet another conflagrationeer—it really has been a long time, Foulk. Ages upon long ages. Have you any idea where I ought to begin looking?"

"More than an idea. You know Nagspeake somewhat, I take it?"

"Fairly well. My colleagues and I pass through from time to time."

Trigemine glanced at the sky again. "It's late to begin the search tonight. What say you to finding a public house for the evening, and then tomorrow we'll start in earnest?"

"Certainly. Where?"

"The Quayside Harbors."

"Ah." Blister smiled. "Very good. Jalap knows the way to the Harbors, don't you, fellow?" He gave the pony another flick with the reins, then wound them around one ankle and picked up the banjo. "Listen, Foulk. Here's a ditty I've been practicing. I very nearly have it down to memory. See if you recognize it."

Trigemine pressed the space between his eyes again as the twanging began once more. "Delighted, friend."

TWO

THE STAINED-GLASS HOUSE

"THERE." Lucy's father put an arm around her shoulders. "Look, now. Didn't I tell you it was splendid?"

Splendid. She hugged her parcels to her chest and forced her face into something less like a scowl, for her father's sake. *Splendid* was not the word she would have used.

Oh, the house was fine, as houses went. It even gave her the slightest feeling of familiarity, though she couldn't quite work out why. But it was still a *house,* and Lucy could not forgive it for that. It had no bow, no masts, no water frothing alongside the hull it also didn't have. The clouds overhead weren't sails but vapor, and they were no comfort at all. In fact, sweeping over this unfamiliar roof instead of over the beautiful geometry of a ship's rigging, they made everything worse. What did clouds matter on land?

A house was not a home. Only a ship could ever be that for

Lucy Bluecrowne. And not just any ship, but Lucy's ship, the topsail schooner *Left-Handed Fate*. The schooner that had been her home since she was five years old.

And yet here she stood, staring at this house that, to add insult to injury, sat high above the nearest bit of water—which was not even the sea but a fast-moving, muddy brown river rushing along somewhere out of sight down below. And although Nagspeake wasn't America per se, it was still on the coast of the American continent: another place that Lucy, born outside London and raised among British tars, could never conceive of as home.

It wasn't an ugly house—that much she had to admit, even if it didn't properly resemble any dwelling she'd ever seen before. It was tall and narrow, and the effect was rather more like a bell tower that had been plopped on *top* of a house than like a house at all. There were all manner of windows: leaded-glass bow windows on either side of the front door, windows pieced together from circles of crown glass like bull's-eyes, and stained-glass windows that flared in jewel tones. Chimneys rose on the east and west walls.

But—another mark against it—it was a thumping great *huge* house, far bigger than the Bluecrowne residence in England, where they occasionally spent some time ashore. Lucy thought wistfully of the tiny cabin, shaped like a wedge cut from a short, fat cake, that had been her quarters aboard the *Fate* for seven of her twelve years. How on earth could something as huge as this house be comfortable? It would be drafty, it would be empty, it would echo . . .

"Come, look closer." Lucy's father tugged her across the broad lawn. "I want to show you first, before Xiaoming and Liao get here."

She could hear it in his voice: He knew exactly what she was thinking. Lucy considered trying a bit harder to seem cheerful and discarded the idea straight away. He knew, had *always* known, just exactly what she thought of the plan this house was part of. He was the one asking her to leave the *Fate*. It was for him to comfort Lucy, not the other way around, even if this meant behaving like an ordinary father and not at all like Captain Richard Bluecrowne, owner and master of a storied letter-of-marque, a privateering schooner so fearsome that no vessel on the Atlantic dared cross her.

He strode up the stairs and fumbled in his pocket for a key. "Garvett and Kendrick and the rest were here for a good while yesterday. Hopefully they've put the place all a-tanto." Lucy followed him inside. There was nothing to say.

Captain Bluecrowne stalked through the dim space, lighting candles and lamps. Lucy found a table and set down her belongings. She waited in a patch of strange red-green light, the result of the deep scarlet sunset slicing through a window pieced together from hues of jade. That window and several others, heirloom stained glass, had come all the way from the residence in England, most likely so Lucy would feel more at home here. All that the familiar glass managed to do was to remind her that even the house in England was now gone.

"There," her father announced at last. "See how splendid our old windows look! You wouldn't think a room so big could be so cozy, would you?"

"No," Lucy said frankly. It was a nice enough parlor, but it was far too big to be cozy. In fact, the entire parlor floor seemed to be one giant room. "It's so . . ."

Her father nodded. "It was my suggestion to keep it quite open. I thought, after all those years living in such a small space —" He stopped speaking, and Lucy pressed her lips together to keep from shrieking that she *loved* those small spaces, that he *knew* she loved them, that it would have been far wiser *not* to expect her to be immediately enchanted by a place that was the exact *opposite* of everything she loved and was being made to leave behind.

"You can choose which room you'd like for your own quarters," Captain Bluecrowne said, a little helplessly.

Lucy swallowed. "All right."

For a moment they looked mutely at each other. If they hadn't already gone round and round about this plan, over and over again for months during the voyage from Tor Bay to China to Nagspeake, Lucy might've spoken up then and begged him one last time not to maroon her. *Don't make me stay, Papa. I'll die here. I'll die without the deck under my feet, without the song of the rigging in my ears. I'll die without you, without the crew, without the schooner, without the sea.*

Perhaps she spoke out loud without realizing it. Perhaps her father just knew. "Lucy—"

The front door swung open, and the small, thin shape of her

seven-year-old half brother darted inside. He stopped in the center of the room, staring in awe at the green stained-glass window still bleeding sunset onto the floor. "So beautiful," he breathed. "Isn't it beautiful, Lucy?"

"Yes," she said, finally forcing cheer into her face and voice. Guilting her papa was one thing. Making her brother sad was another. "Yes, it's very pretty. What's that in the Chinese, Liao?"

"Hěn piàoliang," Liao replied. Then he dashed back out the door and returned, tugging on the hand of a tall and slender, dark-eyed woman who wore her long brown hair twisted up behind her head and secured with carved ornaments: Liao's mother, and Lucy's stepmother. The crew called her Lady Xiaoming, but it hadn't seemed appropriate for Lucy to use her given name, so after much discussion, Lucy and Xiaoming had settled on Jìmǔ. *Stepmother,* basically, although somehow it sounded nicer to Lucy in Chinese than in English.

Lucy had been certain when they'd first met that anyone so very lovely and so very unlike herself would be remote and haughty and strange. She'd been even younger then than Liao was now, and her first long voyage was the one that had carried her to the seaside village on the other side of the world, there to meet the woman her father had fallen in love with.

She'd been prepared to hate Xiaoming and to resent the tiny sibling she'd never met. It wasn't that she was resisting the replacement of her own mother; Caroline Bluecrowne had died when Lucy was only a few months old. It was simply that she was certain these two foreigners could never be proper family. But although Lucy hated being wrong and hated admitting to it even more, she'd realized almost immediately that she'd been mistaken. After that she'd begun to look forward to the *Left-Handed Fate*'s journeys to China. Now, six years later, she loved both Xiaoming and Liao desperately. It seemed they had been family ever since that first meeting, even though the actual marriage of her father and Xiaoming had taken place only a few months before, on the journey here to Nagspeake.

Even Nagspeake was spoiled for her now, Lucy realized. Captain Bluecrowne had chosen it for the location of the new family home because it was one of the few places on the Atlantic that had kept its neutrality during the wars between England and France. She'd always enjoyed their visits to the city before, but that had been when they were temporary stops. *Now I shall never be able to love this place again,* she thought glumly.

Xiaoming paused in the doorway to step out of her shoes, then cast her eyes around the room. When she'd first come aboard the *Left-Handed Fate,* she had brought a small trunk full of beautiful things: gowns, boxy tunics, and flowing trousers of satins and silks embellished with medallions and flowers. After a few days aboard, though, she had enlisted Lucy (who actually rather liked dresses but also liked to be able to climb the rigging) to help her work out a more ship-friendly wardrobe. Today she wore some of these garments, which resembled a sailor's suit of blue cotton except for the yellow ribbons sewn in the seams of the trousers and the matching chrysanthemums the sailmaker—who was particularly vain about his embroidery—had stitched all over the tunic.

Her eyes came to rest on Lucy. "And so?" she asked. "Will it do?"

Fortunately, Lucy's face was still in its false, cheerful-for-Liao's-sake configuration. "Yes, ma'am. Just prime."

Her stepmother looked at her as if she knew exactly how big a lie this was. But she said nothing, just reached out and scratched Lucy's shoulder gently—once, twice—with her index and middle fingers. When they had first met, Lucy, much younger, had been obsessed with the sailors' habit of scratching the backstays in the ship's rigging for luck, and she'd gone around scratching everything, just in case. Xiaoming, amused, had begun scratching Lucy, ostensibly also for luck. The gesture had persisted. Now it meant something like luck but also something like love.

"Come and see this window!" Liao bounded to the one that faced the hillside, and reached up to touch the stained glass. "There's a picture in it!"

"Each one is different," Lucy's father said, smiling. "Lucy will tell you about them sometime, perhaps. They come from Broadyew Cottage."

"That was your house in the countryside?"

Was. Lucy cringed.

"What's this one's story?" Liao asked, examining the window with his face scarcely an inch from the glass. Then he leaned closer still, pressing his nose right up against a patch of emerald and his index finger next to it. "Is that it, Papa? Will that be the workshop?"

"Workshop?" Lucy joined him at the window. "What workshop?"

"*My* workshop." He pointed at a red stone outbuilding that

peeked out of the pinewoods on the hill. "Since I wasn't allowed to work on my rockets properly on the ship." Liao glanced over his shoulder. "Is that the one, Papa? May I go and see?"

"Certainly. It's yours, if you decide it will do. I believe Mr. Harrick had some of your stores brought up." Captain Bluecrowne smiled. "I suppose you'd like to have a look at that before the rest of the house?"

"Yes, please, may I look at the workshop first?" Liao asked, all but hopping in place in his excitement.

"Yes, you may, but —"

Lucy didn't hear the rest. Liao dragged her out of the house, hauling on her hand all the way to the red stone hutch. It took both of them to work open the heavy wooden door. The smell of gunpowder shot immediately up her nose. It wasn't unlike standing in the powder magazine aboard the *Fate*.

Liao inhaled deeply as he took in the space and the crates that had been brought up from the schooner. "It's perfect," he whispered.

Lucy shook her head. "You're going to blow up the house one of these days."

"I am not," he said, nettled.

"Just make sure I'm out of it when you do."

"I won't blow up the house, Lucy! I never blew up the ship, did I? *Did I?*"

"Only because Papa said you couldn't fire rockets aboard any longer."

"Because of *one little fire*. One little fire, and it wasn't even my fault. It was a bad powder charge! *My* powder charges never go bad!"

Liao had a near-obsessive love of pyrotechnics, which had been something like a family business for his mother's ancestors for generations, and he had come aboard the *Fate* already knowing more than most of the gunner's mates about gunpowder and what it could do. Lucy was accustomed to lads Liao's age running about acting as ship's boys and powder monkeys, but it *had* been a little strange the first time the gunner had asked her brother's opinion on ways to fancy up the salutes to be fired for Coronation Day.

And heavens above, had Liao *delivered*. The great guns of the *Left-Handed Fate* had painted the water with spurts of flame in colors that had made the gun crews cross themselves: lilacs and crimsons and melting golds, and blues like Mediterranean water.

And now he had a whole workshop of his own in which to mess about with explosives.

"Just make sure I'm out of the house," Lucy repeated airily.

Liao set down a grinding mortar he'd taken from one of the crates. He gave her a thoughtful look. "Will you be happy here, Lucy?"

She studied him for a moment. "I'm not sure," she said at last, deciding to err on the side of honesty. "But if I'm not, Liao, it isn't because of you, you know."

"Mm." He put the mortar on a shelf, then took it down again and put it on a different one. "I miss home," he added. "Even though I like you and Papa and the ship and the crew and everyone."

"That's precisely the thing." Lucy sat on a keg and rubbed her hands through her short blond hair. "If I were a boy I should be a midshipman now, and Papa would have no reason to put me ashore."

"I didn't think you could be a midshipman on a mark-letter ship," Liao said. "You told me that, I think."

"Well, I would be *like* a midshipman, then. But part of the crew, certainly. Properly part of it, and assigned to a watch. And the *Fate* is a *letter-of-marque,* Liao, not a *mark-letter,* and also a *schooner,* not a *ship.*"

Liao rolled his eyes. "You know what I meant." He turned back to his crate and disappeared into it from the waist up for a moment. Then he straightened, his brow furrowed. "Lucy, if it mattered to be a boy, wouldn't I stay aboard?"

She reached over and brushed packing straw from his hair. "Do you want to be a sailor?"

"No," Liao replied immediately. "I like to sail, but this is what I like best." He waved his hand around the room. "Making fireworks."

"Well, there you have it." Halfway through the remark she realized she had no good answer to the question that would logically follow it: *If Papa wants us to be able to do what we like best, why can't you be a sailor?*

Liao was silent for a moment, and Lucy was certain he was

trying to work through that puzzle for himself. Mercifully, however, he decided not to ask. Instead, his eyes went crafty. "We could sneak you back aboard! Just as we snuck Mr. Fitch's boarding party onto the ship in that harbor in the Adriatic Sea."

"It was a *brig*, Liao, and I absolutely cannot sneak aboard the *Fate*, no matter how much I should like to. I cannot go without Papa's permission. A seaman can't run about refusing the captain's orders each time they don't suit his opinions."

"No, of course not. I wasn't thinking of it as an *order*."

"Well, it is." Neither had Lucy thought of it that way at first, but once it had occurred to her to do so, she'd decided this was the only way to look at it. A child might disobey her father and remain his beloved daughter, but a sailor couldn't go about disobeying the captain and expect to remain a part of that crew. And in her heart, even if no one else believed it, Lucy would always be a sailor.

Liao reached for the end of his queue, the long, plaited pigtail that hung down his back. Technically he didn't have to wear one any longer, now that he wasn't living in China, but the moment the boy had seen how vain the sailors were about their own pigtails and how impressed they were with his, Liao had decided he absolutely had to keep his braid. Now he worried it between his fingers as he thought things through. "Well, if I can have a workshop," he said at last, "then you ought to have a boat."

Lucy laughed. "What would I do with a boat? The harbor's miles away."

"Float it in the river," Liao replied, as if this were the most obvious thing in the world. "The river's not far."

"I can't sail a boat on my own."

"A little boat, you could. I've seen you do it. Or you could teach me to help you. I could be the first mate. And the gunner," he added, gazing thoughtfully at the keg of powder Lucy was sitting on. "We should need at least one gun, but only for firing salutes." As much as he loved gunnery, Liao hated actual battles—another reason he could never be a proper sailor.

Reluctantly, Lucy considered. Would it be anything like the same, sailing on the river Skidwrack when she was accustomed to great open waters like the Mediterranean and the Atlantic? Plainly not. And the vessel would have to be something quite little for Lucy to be able to handle it on her own. A jolly boat, a gig, perhaps a small cutter . . .

"It's not the worst idea you've ever had," she admitted at length. It wouldn't replace what she was losing in the *Fate*—nothing was going to replace that—but it would mean having an escape from dry land when she needed one.

Liao beamed, looking terribly pleased with himself. "I shall make up a very special rocket to set off for our first voyage," he declared. "I'll start work straight away."

"Well, I haven't gotten the thing yet," Lucy grumbled.

"You haven't a boat yet, but you have a *plan*. I tell you what, Lucy. Let's have a rocket right now! To celebrate the plan. Perhaps something in green," Liao said. He dived back into the crate.

She smiled despite herself. "This very minute? We shall barely be able to see it."

"It doesn't matter if we can see it." He turned with a rocket half his own height grasped in his arms. "We'll know it's there. And we'll *hear* it," he added with relish. He grabbed her hand with the few fingers he could spare while cradling the explosive, and pulled her outside. "*Everyone's* going to hear it."

THREE

THE IRONMONGER

THIS place is miserable," Trigemine observed, stepping down from the wagon and eyeing the darkening Quayside Harbors from the line of blue pines at the bottom of the hill. Here the district was a mixture of stone and wooden buildings, nearly all of them embellished with flourishes of Nagspeake's warped and twisted old iron: fences, lampposts, even ornamental gingerbread-work that hung from the eaves of some of the buildings like creeping ivy. Nearer to the water the stone structures thinned out and the wooden ones multiplied and spilled onto the piers.

"Miserable?" Blister said, eyeing his companion sidelong. "After what you've seen, *this* is miserable?"

"I don't like the water, and this entire place appears likely to fall in at any moment. But yes, you're right. I suppose I've seen proper misery, and this isn't it."

Blister stepped down and faced the Harbors. His eyes had gone sharp. "I smell powder."

"Well, it's the smugglers' neck of town."

"Not just black powder," he said in an absent tone that was completely at odds with his focused expression. "This is something else. Something fancier. Something . . ." The pony nosed his chest. He shoved its face aside and sniffed the air. "Can't tell what. But whatever it is, it's not wafting into town from yesterday's gunnery practice."

At that very moment, there was a tremendous, percussive bang from somewhere to the west. As one, Trigemine and Blister turned to see a tangle of silver-green trails and tendrils of smoke breaking apart in the sky.

"Oh, yes." Blister grinned. "Nicely done, Foulk. I believe our conflagrationeer's in town after all."

Trigemine made a short bow. "I did tell you so."

"Tomorrow I shall head up to see what's to be seen on that hill. And your man? Whoever has the other item you were hoping to acquire for Morvengarde?"

"Oh, I *know* my man's here. You said you're familiar with the Harbors?"

"Certainly. I used to keep a warehouse here, ages and ages back."

"Then perhaps you might recommend a place where we can find rooms."

"I could do. The building where I used to keep my warehouse, in fact. The Quenching Press, I think it's called now." Blister took the pony by its bridle and started walking. "This way."

"The Quenching Press?" Trigemine repeated thoughtfully. "Well, that's convenient. That's where I was going to begin looking for the Ironmonger."

Blister stopped and turned with an odd expression on his face. "The Ironmonger?"

For the second time, Trigemine felt a touch of satisfaction at Blister's discomfiture. "You've heard of him." This didn't precisely come as a surprise. The roaming world was a small place, and the man known as the Ironmonger was special. Trigemine waited, but Blister said nothing more, just gave the pony's harness a tug to get him moving again.

They hiked along the edge of town, more or less parallel to the water. The tavern, it turned out, was impossible to miss. It stood midway between the blue pines and the gray-upon-gray of the rest of the town: a four-story warehouse of stone the color of roan foxes. Huge pairs of black wooden doors ran around the first story. One set stood open to the day, letting reddening sunlight in and voices out.

Blister hitched the pony to a post and gestured up at the lintel. The names BLISTER AND BURNS were carved into the stone, along with a date in the previous century. "That's nice," he said, grinning broadly.

"Maybe it'll be good for a free pint."

"Maybe!" Blister grabbed the banjo from the front of the wagon and played a triumphant flourish—or at least Trigemine assumed that was what it was meant to be.

"Well, see what you can do about that, and about rooms. I want to have a look around."

Inside, four stories overhead, a huge skylight in the pressed copper ceiling poured sunset down onto the tavern, which took up the entire first floor. At the corners of the space, four lift cages hung from thick cables. These lifts gave access to three levels of galleries lined with smaller black doors. Some had shingles hanging beside them that announced businesses, and others were secured with huge bolts and locks. The ones on the second floor were smaller and had brass numbers affixed to them, and Trigemine figured these were the tavern's rooms for hire.

The current collection of customers was a varied lot: Nagspeake had its own prejudices, but it was a sailors' town, and what mattered here were the differences between able seamen, ordinary ones, and officers, not the differences between skin tones and physiognomies. The Quenching Press bore this out: scattered about the room was a handful of assorted white folks and an equal number of folks who weren't. At a cursory glance, Trigemine thought a few were probably of Native extraction, three or four were probably African, and a couple might've been from farther east—the Philippines, perhaps, or maybe even China, though Trigemine was pretty sure even in Nagspeake it was early in the century to be meeting many Chinese on this particular bit of North American coast. Almost as strange to Trigemine was the scattering of trousered women among the clientele, a couple of whom were plainly regulars here.

He strolled through the raucous clutter of servers and dining furniture and patrons toward an empty table near one of the lifts.

The place smelled not unpleasantly of chowder and roast meat and malty, hoppy beer, and beneath that was the ever-present Nagspeake odor of water, stone, lichen, pine, and warm metal.

His figuring had told him that the Quenching Press would be the best place for crossing paths with the Ironmonger, and he knew that this was roughly the right time. Between them, Trigemine and the kairos mechanism could manage pinpoint accuracy, but since the main purpose for the visit to Nagspeake was Blister's conflagrationeer, Trigemine had been happy to settle for rough calculations about the Ironmonger. He didn't figure he'd bump into the man tonight. Which was just fine, considering walking through time really did take it out of a fellow. What he really wanted was food, beer, bed, and to start work in the morning.

Trigemine dropped into a chair and took off his hat. He stretched, leaned back, and immediately knocked into the man at the next table. Turning to apologize, he found himself staring into the face of very person he'd come to find.

Even seated, the Ironmonger was tall, and he was broad with muscle. His face was a deep burnished brown; his eyes were darker yet, and they were not amused. A dull pink scar emerged from his collar and wound its way around from somewhere on his right shoulder up across his neck to his left ear. One hand, callused and scattered with shiny burn scars, rested on the table in front of him.

Trigemine murmured a smooth apology and turned away. The Ironmonger it was for certain, but he wasn't alone, and the other man at the table, the one whose gaze was hidden behind a pair of spectacles . . . well, anyone else in the tavern might have glanced at him and forgotten the fellow a heartbeat later, but Trigemine had done enough wandering to know trouble when he saw it.

As he considered the presence of the second man and began a set of furious mental reckonings, Blister plunked into the vacant seat opposite Trigemine and waved a pair of keys at him. "Last two! Take your pick."

Trigemine took the key marked *8* and raised it to his lips. "Shhh." He flicked his eyes toward the Ironmonger's table. Blister leaned sideways with agonizing slowness to peer past Trigemine at the man who sat behind him. Then he straightened again, his eyes curious.

"Who's the other?" he whispered. Trigemine shook his head. There was no way he was saying a damned thing out loud until those two were gone.

Fortunately a server chose that moment to appear, and while Blister ordered as much food as the little table was likely to hold, Trigemine leaned back again to try to pick the conversation at the next table out of the general tavern noise.

The Ironmonger was speaking, and his voice was deep and rich and bitter. "It took fighting against the States to be able to walk free. Is it so different a place now that I ought to forgive it after so short a time? To say nothing of binding myself to it."

"It isn't the States I'm asking you to bind yourself to," the man in the spectacles said. "I'm not asking you to bind yourself to any-thing, actually."

"Except you," the Ironmonger noted. "Why else would you seek me out to ask me to join you in some nothing town in the middle of Louisiana Territory?"

Out of the corner of his eye, Trigemine saw the bespectacled man shrug. "It's a *crossroads* town," he said, "and it needs a blacksmith. It's an invitation; accept it or don't, it's entirely up to you. Either way, my offer for the Albatross stands."

Trigemine stiffened. *My workings are never this far wrong,* he thought wildly. He reached into his watch pocket and from the pincushion he plucked an engraved pin like the one he'd given Blister. There was no way things would go well if he resorted to any sort of scene here. He rolled the pin between his thumb and forefinger thoughtfully. But in another moment, somewhere else . . .

Rapidly, silently, he began running numbers again. Chronometric trigonometry wasn't something you did in your head or by counting on your fingers, and despite his expertise, Trigemine felt acid panic rise in his gut at the idea of dragging anyone out of the here-and-now at a moment's notice. He was hugely relieved when the Ironmonger finally replied with some impatience, "I said I would think about it."

The other man stood. "You know how to find me, when you decide on either question." No answer from the Ironmonger, and a moment later the bespectacled man passed Trigemine's table en route to the door. Trigemine watched him all the way across the tavern, until he disappeared into the falling night.

Blister's eyes goggled. *"Was that what I think —"*

"I believe so." Trigemine stuck the pin back in its pincushion. Then he slid out of his chair and ducked around to the other table just as the Ironmonger was rising to leave. Trigemine made a short bow. "Christopher Swifte, I think? May I join you?"

The Ironmonger considered him without expression. "I wondered." He nodded shortly at the empty chair.

Trigemine sat and extended a hand. "Foulk Trigemine."

Christopher Swifte's grip, predictably enough, was crushing, and not out of friendliness or enthusiasm. "You're one of Morvengarde's creatures, aren't you?"

Creatures. He'd used the term himself earlier, but Trigemine didn't much like hearing it applied to himself. "I am *employed* by Mr. Morvengarde, yes."

Swifte gave a little snort. "I hear that's not how he usually sees it."

Trigemine let that one pass. It was true enough, anyway. "I'm in the market for your services. Are you selling?"

"That's what I do," Swifte said shortly. "I make weapons, and I sell them."

"I'm in the market for one weapon in particular. Sounds like I'm not the only one."

The Ironmonger reached into his jacket and, with a soft, hollow noise of metal on leather, brought out the knife called the Albatross. He set it on the table between them.

The Albatross was terrifying and beautiful. It was made all of metal, from curved tip to handle: gleaming watered steel for the blade, black iron for the grip. The handle was fashioned with a raised pattern of feathers and a knob in the shape of two webbed feet curled against each other. Where a longer blade might have worn its hilt, this knife had a swelling in the shape of a bird's skull. The blade itself, with its waves of lighter and darker metal, resembled a long, viciously hooked beak. The whole thing was about the length of a man's forearm.

"It's a work of art," Trigemine said. Disturbing art, certainly, but art nonetheless.

"So the Jumper said too." Swifte lifted his mug and regarded him over the rim.

"He *was* a Jumper, then." Trigemine smiled thinly. *Damn and hellfire take him, whoever he is.* "I thought as much. And will you sell it to him?"

"I haven't decided."

"May I ask why not? I'm prepared to make a generous offer, but I'd like to know if there's one on the table needing to be beat."

"It isn't a question of beating his offer. It's a question of whether I want to deal with him. Or, I suppose now, whether I want to deal with *you*. Or Morvengarde." Swifte took the knife, slid it back into its sheath, and smoothed his lapel down over it. "What's your proposal? Your boss doesn't generally deal in simple transactions."

It was ever so slightly unnerving, the way Swifte managed to talk about Morvengarde without that ripple of unease that even Blister had betrayed. It put Trigemine a little on edge. And once again, the Ironmonger's comment was completely accurate.

"That he does not," Trigemine admitted. "Although I suppose if the only deal to be made was the outright purchase of this particular blade, I'd make it. But what we really want is to secure your services on an extended basis."

"I'll make no contracts."

"No contracts," Trigemine said quickly. "A gentleman's agreement for twenty blades like this one. But I imagine that'll take some time."

"Twenty years, easy, if you'd like them to have the properties of this blade as well as the look of it. And by way of payment?"

Trigemine spread his hands. "Name your price."

"For twenty blades, and twenty years' dealings with your boss." Swifte tilted his chair back. "That'll take some calculating. And there's the Jumper to think of."

Yes, there is, Trigemine thought sourly. But he kept his face neutral. "Where can I find you?"

"I'm staying with another metalsmith in town, a fellow called Forgeron. You can find me at his workshop, though I'd prefer you didn't."

"I'll wait to hear from you, then. I'm staying upstairs. Number eight."

"All right." Christopher Swifte drained what remained in his mug and stood. He had to be nearly seven feet tall. "Mr. Trigemine."

"Mr. Swifte."

The Ironmonger departed, and Trigemine returned to his own table, where a pair of frothy mugs and a bread barge had arrived.

Blister looked up from a roll he'd split and spread with honey. "That is an . . . imposing man."

Trigemine sighed and reached for a fork. "This is not going the way I'd expected."

"Damned Jumpers," Blister said sympathetically.

"Have you met many?"

"Five."

"That's five more Jumpers than I'd recommend to anyone."

The peddler chewed thoughtfully. "I don't know, actually. They're interesting. Unpredictable, which is a very rare thing in this world."

"I don't care for unpredictability," Trigemine muttered.

"No, I imagine you don't. Did I hear him say something about someone named Forgeron?" Blister's voice was unnaturally casual.

"He did. Why?"

Blister shook his head. "Nothing, really. Eat," he said, pushing the basket of rolls across the table. "They'll get cold."

FOUR

SPLINTERS

IRE as they bear!

The noise was like thunder and earthquake and the splitting of great rocks under the hammer of a giant. Light stabbed outward in tongues of crimson flame, visible only here and there through the breaks in the deep swirling smoke that hid most of the world. The smell alone was enough to send the pulse racing: acrid and full of the tang of hot metal and burnt rag and powder. Then the smoke was rushing away aft, clearing just in time to show the return broadside from the frigate across the water: eighteen fiery spurting licks from eighteen great guns, near-perfectly synchronized and too close to miss.

Down!

Lucy went down hard on her stomach as the unmistakable whipping whine of grapeshot screeched overhead: thousands of small iron balls slicing through the air at body height, crashing into the masts, slamming into the deck, kicking up splinters the size and shape of daggers and broadswords.

There were cries; people had been hit. Lucy raised her head and stared into the wide, dead eyes of John Backell, sponger of the number three gun crew. His face slid rapidly from her as someone dragged his body off and heaved it overboard and out of the way through the nearest gun port. The corpse left a fat slick of red in its wake, and then it was gone. It wasn't the only one.

Lucy shoved herself to her feet, scrambling a bit to keep her footing on the scarlet-slippery deck. She grabbed Backell's abandoned sponge, a long stick with a roll of wet sheep's wool at the end, from where it had fallen. *I can help. I can sponge. I can do it.*

Someone grabbed her by the collar and flung her back, yanking the sponge from her grip.

Get her below. Lucy, go to the cockpit.

The cockpit, where Dr. Domanova would be working on the injured. *I can do more than thread silk for stitches,* Lucy argued. *I can fight—I know how! Let me sponge the gun.* But stronger hands were moving her toward the companionway, and their owner ignored her protests.

Then: *Fire!*

The second broadside rang out, and Lucy lost her footing as she was shoved at the companion ladder. Down she went, arse over teakettle like a lubber with no sea legs. She crawled behind the ladder and hid, her face wet and burning. She was smarting from the pain and the far worse humiliation of the fall, and unbearably angry at being treated like a mere passenger to be got out of the way.

Someone came clattering down the ladder, stopped at the bottom, turned a fast circle, and found her hiding there. She recognized the face, but somehow couldn't put a name to it. The strangeness of that was enough to catch her attention. How could she not bring forth the man's name? It was like forgetting the name of an uncle.

He caught her by the wrist and hauled her out from behind the rungs. Lucy slipped on blood and instinctively looked upward. There had been blood on the decks, but enough to come pouring down the hatch?

There was no blood on the ladder, but there was blood under her feet.

Her head swam suddenly and she nearly crumpled. The nameless man picked her up in his arms as if she were a much smaller child, and once again the dizziness came washing over her.

Come now, no more arguing. You saw what that splinter did to Backell. Let's give Dr. Domanova a peep at that gash, make sure it ain't worse nor it looks.

Gash? Lucy looked down at her body as the sailor carried her to the surgeon. Her dress, knotted up over a pair of nankeen trousers, was splashed with scarlet. Not little splashes, either. She followed the pattern of the stain up the bodice until she lost it somewhere in the vicinity of her collar and her peripheral vision would show her no more. But by then she could feel her heartbeat in her head, and there was a roaring, thudding pain spreading through her that seemed to have its origins near her left eye.

She put her hand to her temple and felt wetness and a strange uneven edge beneath it. A gaping wound longer than her own palm, and pain.

Easy now.

She screamed.

Fortunately, it wasn't a real scream this time, only a strangled cry that was just enough to jolt Lucy out of the dream and into the present, jarring her awake in her new and unfamiliar, too flat and too stable bed. Not that anyone was likely to hear a girl's shout in this giant house. That was something to be grateful for, anyhow.

She put her fingers to her forehead and felt for the nearly invisible scar that was all that remained of the damage the splinter had done a year ago. If not for that splinter . . . Lucy had been injured plenty of times; that was part of life aboard a letter-of-marque in wartime, and she had never really known a time when Britain was not at war. But that splinter had very nearly done real, permanent damage.

Now, of course, she knew that the man who'd carried her to the cockpit was her father's coxswain, Kendrick, and that she'd misplaced his name because she'd gone woozy from blood loss. By the time her father had come thundering below to see her, Lucy had been asleep, dosed with a dozen or so drops of laudanum. To hear Captain Bluecrowne tell it, between the laudanum and the blood that nobody'd had time to clean off yet, she'd appeared more dead than alive. That was the moment when he had decided his daughter was finished with privateering and he had begun to concoct this hateful plan to turn her into a landsman.

Lucy sat up, leaned her elbows on her knees, and took a deep breath. Outside the gable window the sky was slate-toned. It was probably sometime at the end of the graveyard watch, or in the first part of the morning watch. But without the sea and the schooner and the bells that structured its day, this sky told her nothing.

The house told her nothing, either. Its creaks were unfamiliar, like words in a foreign language written down with no voice, face, or gestures to help give them meaning. She put a hand on the window-sill and felt nothing but dead wood under a coat of paint. Not like touching any part of the *Fate*. Lay a hand on it anywhere—the gunwale, the tiller, the cordage of a backstay stretching aloft to support a sail—and a ship *spoke*, if one only understood how to listen. Lucy knew how to heed the voice of her schooner. But if this house had anything to tell, it wasn't speaking to her.

At last, with a sigh, she squinted at the clock on the desk, which stood uncomfortably far across the room. It was nearly five: two bells in the morning watch, if there had been ship's bells to toll the watches here. She fell back against her pillows. Wide awake, nothing to do, three hours until breakfast by proper naval standards. Meanwhile, down below in the district on the river, the schooner would be alive with motion. The galley fires would be coming to life. In a few minutes the washing and polishing of the deck would begin, and it would've been the noise of the holystones scraping at the planks that woke her instead of a nightmare. A tear escaped, and Lucy wiped it away angrily as she climbed out of bed.

Beside the clock sat a gift from the crew, which she'd been given the day before but hadn't opened. She picked it up and tore away the brown wrapping and string. Inside was a box, and inside the box was more paper: a stack of fancy watermarked writing paper bound in a green ribbon the same shade as the *Fate*'s hull.

She opened a card that had been tucked into the ribbon and recognized the purser's neat copperplate writing. *To Our Miss Bluecrowne: Never Forget To Write To Us.* A note of thanks written on the new stationery was in order. She sat at the desk, centered a sheet before her, and wondered how to begin. *My dear friends? My dear shipmates?* Or ought she list the Fates by name? *My dear Kendrick, my dear Garvett, my dear Mr. Wooll . . .*

Another drop fell, and this one landed on the page. Lucy blotted it with the sleeve of her nightgown, sniffled, got up, and climbed back into bed. It would never do to spoil such nice paper with tears.

When she woke again, it was just after six-thirty, and even though it was still too early, breakfast smells were wafting through the air. Lucy rolled out of bed, not sure whether she was more annoyed at the idea of breakfast before eight bells or more fascinated that food smells carried at all in a house this big.

She found Xiaoming, Liao, and her father's coxswain in the dining room. Kendrick seemed out of place at the table set with Xiaoming's beautiful heirloom porcelain, especially after the dream Lucy had just woken from. He worked one hand loose from the game of cat's cradle he was playing with Liao and tapped a knuckle to his forehead in good morning.

"I was just about to come and wake you," Xiaoming said. "Breakfast is ready."

"Thank you." Lucy slid onto the bench opposite Liao.

"Morning, Lucy!" the boy sang out. "We get early breakfast, on account of Mr. Garvett has to get back before eight bells. Isn't that splendid?"

"It's different, that's for certain," Lucy said. Kendrick gave her a knowing look as he extracted himself from the tangle of yarn again to reach across the table and pour her coffee. The coffee smelled the same at least, which was a relief. A moment later Garvett came plunging through the kitchen doors with a tray of steaming dishes, and the bacon smelled the same too. Lucy managed a smile.

After the meal she took her cup outside to sit on the top stair of the porch that stretched across the front of the house. The door opened behind her and Xiaoming joined her. "May I sit?"

"*Shì,* Jìmǔ."

"*Xièxiè,*" Xiaoming said with a smile, and sat. For a moment neither of them spoke. "You and I have things in common," she said at last.

"We're both here, I suppose," Lucy said quietly.

She hadn't expected her stepmother to be talking about anything so obvious, but to her surprise, Xiaoming inclined her head in agreement. "We're both here. And furthermore, neither of us is terribly excited about it."

"If you didn't want to come, why didn't you just say so?" Lucy demanded. "Papa wouldn't have made you, would he?"

"No, of course not." Xiaoming laughed. "It is very difficult to make me do anything I don't choose to do." Then she gave Lucy a low-lidded sideways glance. "We are similar that way, as well."

"Then *why?*"

"The first reason, you know. Because I love you and your father, and because he believes this is the best way for us to be a family without being separated by so many seas."

Lucy's cheeks flushed. Xiaoming had always been graceful and kind toward her, but this was the first time she had told Lucy she loved her. And it felt true.

"And the second reason . . ." Xiaoming contemplated the lines of light and shadow on the lawn. "The second reason is that nothing stays the same. Nothing *can*. Time works upon everything, and every morning we wake into a subtly different world than the one we fell asleep in the night before. Nothing stays the same. You have only to turn to the sea you love so much to know this is true."

It wasn't fair, dragging the sea into this, but she was right. No matter how familiar a waterway was, it was impossible to know for certain what the conditions would be on the next voyage that took one there.

"My life has changed more times than you would believe," Xiaoming continued. "When I was a child, my father was . . . an important figure at court, and my life began there. When his days serving the people ended, for many, many years my family lived alone in the mountains. I loved this part of my life. The world below transformed, but for us there were only the change of the seasons and the shifts the sky made in its transit from day into night. And then the emperor gave his people the right to mine the country for metals, which had not previously been permitted, and before long my lonely mountain became a mining village. And the life I had loved became something different."

Lucy listened without interrupting, but what she was thinking was that the only thing worse than being apart from the sea and stuck halfway up a hill would be living at the top of a mountain.

"At first, I hated this invasion of the outside world," Xiaoming said thoughtfully, "but I came to love the new China I discovered. And then many years later, I came to Canton and met your father when the *Left-Handed Fate* stopped there during a voyage, and the world changed again. And then Liao was born, and my choice became clear: Do I remain behind, hoping the things I love will stay unaltered although I know better, or do I become part of the change in the world and take the memory of what I love with me?" She laughed. "And I promise you, not even marrying a Westerner is the biggest or strangest change my life has seen. Nor will it be the last. The things I have seen . . . someday I'll tell you, Lucy, but I doubt you'll believe me."

"That's fine for you," Lucy interrupted. It was terribly rude, but she couldn't help herself. This conversation was poised to turn into a lecture about how she'd understand when she was older and had the wisdom of experience, and she didn't think she could bear one of those just now. "*You* got to choose. If *I* could choose, I wouldn't stop Papa from building this house, or from bringing you and Liao here. I like that we're going to be a family. But why must that mean I can't go back to sea with him?"

Xiaoming sighed. "I understand, but I think no answer I can give would satisfy you. It would be a mother's answer, and you'd like it no better than the one your father gave you. But I will tell you another thing I know, because I am older and wiser than I appear,

and I have seen many revolutions and many transmutations in the world: Those who are desperate to keep things from changing tend to do more damage than good."

She stood up and brushed invisible wrinkles from her trousers. "Do this for Liao and me: Consider what it would take to make this place at least somewhat homelike, even if you think it can never truly be home."

Lucy sat on the step for what felt like a long time after Xiaoming left. She ought to have gone to help Garvett and his mate with the washing-up so they could get back to the *Fate* for the hands' breakfast, but instead she rested her eyes on the line of trees that marked the slope leading down to the river.

What would it take to make this house something like home? She turned the question reluctantly over in her mind. The answer, of course, was that a house could never be home. Therefore, what she wanted was a ship. And a ship was too much for one girl to captain with a crew of a single small boy. A boat it would have to be, then.

She got to her feet and went inside. Kendrick sat at the table, busy with a needle and thread and a half-sewn ditty bag. He looked up as she came to stand beside him. "I'd like to go to the Harbors," Lucy announced. "If this is going to work at all, I shall have to have a barky of my own."

To her surprise, Kendrick grinned. "Hear her," he said, clapping a giant, callused hand on her shoulder. "I think it's the plan of the world." He turned to Xiaoming. "With your permission, madam, I think we can find something suitable without dipping too far into the housekeeping money."

Xiaoming smiled broadly. "Use whatever is necessary, Mr. Kendrick. I should much rather Lucy have the right vessel than worry about whether or not there are curtains."

Lucy's heart glowed for the first time since she'd arrived in Nagspeake, and she rushed around the table to put her arms awkwardly around her stepmother's shoulders. "Thank you, Jìmǔ."

Xiaoming leaned her cheek against Lucy's forehead. "Liao will want to go with you. I believe he's in the workshop."

Lucy nodded and sprinted for the door, shouting her brother's name at the top of her lungs.

FIVE

THE QUAYSIDE HARBORS

KENDRICK put the *Fate*'s gig neatly alongside the wharf. Lucy hopped out and glanced around as she steadied the boat for Liao.

The Quayside Harbors was a tumbledown shambles of a district without, it seemed, a truly vertical wall to be seen anywhere. The buildings had long ago gone gray from exposure to sun and rain and river, and they were built so thickly on the disreputable-looking piers that jutted into the Skidwrack that Lucy couldn't see where they ended and the shore-built part of the quarter began. Breezes wafted in and out between the buildings, carrying the odors of timber and wet stone, mud and river wrack, lichen, mold, minerally metal, and sunbaked canvas. It wasn't the smell of the sea or quite the smell of any other harbor Lucy knew, yet it made her nose twitch and her heart fill with a bittersweet combination of homesickness and joy.

"All right, then," Kendrick called. "This is John Agony Pier. I'll run Garvett and Beller round to the *Fate*, and then my errands ought not to take more 'n an hour. You two can explore a bit and meet me back here, and we'll see about your barky. You have some money?" he asked Lucy.

She patted the purse tied into her pocket. "I have."

"And you've got your whistle."

"Yes," she said impatiently. She wore the brass bosun's whistle anytime she went ashore, but she was always mildly annoyed when Kendrick checked to be sure she had it. Once the *Fate* left, who would come if she whistled, anyhow?

All in a moment, Lucy's feelings about the whistle changed, and she clutched it through the fabric of her shirt.

Satisfied, the coxswain touched his knuckle to his temple. "Good exploring, then." He cast the gig off, and Lucy and Liao were on their own.

"He could have gone straight to the *Fate*," Liao said as they watched Kendrick depart. "We could have explored from there."

"I asked him not to."

"Why? Don't you want to visit the ship?"

"More than anything, but I was afraid it would make me too homesick to be excited about our boat," Lucy admitted.

"Mm." Liao nodded wisely. Then he brightened. "What shall we do first?"

"Let's just walk around a bit, see what there is to see." There was a charming launch moored not far from where they stood, just a little ways down the pier. It was probably too big for Lucy, but she wanted a closer look anyway.

"All right."

The quays were lined with small craft, and for a while they just wandered up and down, Lucy explaining what they were seeing, Liao looking politely wherever she gestured.

"That's a pretty little barge. Lateen rigged—see the long yard there?"

"That boat isn't big enough for a gun," Liao said critically. "Not even a small one."

"Even small guns are too heavy for any boat you and I could sail, Liao. You shall have to content yourself with rockets."

His face fell. "Oh."

They walked on. "There's a gig. Clinker-built—do you see how the boards in the hull overlap? Not like that launch there, with the boards all flush. That's carvel-built. She's near thirty feet," Lucy said wistfully. "I suppose she's too big."

"Buying?"

They turned toward the voice. Lucy, expecting to see an old salt chewing on an unlit cigar, blinked in surprise. The man who'd spoken sat against a piling, one leg dangling off the pier. Before him was a wooden tool chest that doubled as a workbench, against which he'd propped a painted sign: LOCKS OPENED WHILE YOU WAIT. On the chest sat a small casket, and the man busily picking its lock with the ease of long experience. . . . Was he *Chinese?*

"Buying?" he asked again, eyes on his work.

Nagspeake was home to sailors from all over the world, but Lucy couldn't remember having met anyone else from China here before. Liao, just as surprised as Lucy, darted over to him, launching immediately into his first language. The locksmith set down his tools and scratched his head before replying, also in Chinese— though Lucy thought he spoke it with an accent that was different from Liao and his mother's.

Liao's face burst into a smile. This time Lucy picked out his name and hers in his reply. He turned back to her. "Just think, Lucy, this fellow's parents came to Nagspeake when he was your age! And from Acapulco!"

"Manila Galleon?" Lucy guessed. Until fairly recently the galleons going back and forth between Manila and Acapulco had been nearly the only way the West traded with China, and almost all the Chinese sailors Lucy had ever met had served on one of those ships.

"Very good guess," he said, switching to English and sounding surprised, possibly even impressed. "Both of my grandfathers were sailors on the Manila route, before the one quit and took up locksmithing instead." He set aside his work. "Your brother says you're looking for a boat."

"Perhaps," Lucy said, making her face carefully neutral.

"We should like something big enough for a very small gun," Liao said politely. "If you please."

The man considered the two of them with raised eyebrows. "A gunboat, is it? Who for?"

"For me," Lucy said a little defensively. "Only it needn't be a gunboat."

"It will be, too," Liao interjected. "It will be a *rocket* boat if it won't hold a gun."

"We are looking for something in the way of a gig or a launch," Lucy said. "Twenty feet or so."

"Twenty feet? And you figure you'll sail it?" He sounded amused, but not completely disbelieving. "You know how to sail?"

Lucy would've settled for giving him a glare that let him know exactly how insulting that question was. Liao, apparently, felt the situation demanded words. "Certainly she does! Lucy knows everything about boats and such."

"Does she, now?" The locksmith considered Lucy for a moment. "As it happens, I do know a few coves looking to sell." He fumbled in his pocket and came up with a scrap of paper and a pencil, then unfolded a blade from the tool he'd been using before, scraped the lead to a point, and jotted a few lines. "Here. Start with Tom Yarrow, there," he said as he held out the little page, and tapped the top name with the end of his pencil. "He's just on the next pier over. Young fellow. Anyone can tell you where he docks. His barky isn't quite twenty feet. Might suit. If you find him, tell him Jianming Cerrajero sent you. We've shipped together once or twice. Mention my name and maybe he won't try to gouge you on the price too badly."

"Jianming?" Liao repeated with a grin. "Your name sounds a bit like my mother's name, Mr. Cerrajero."

The locksmith was not amused. "Which is what?"

"Xiaoming, though our other name is Bluecrowne."

Mr. Cerrajero gave Liao a dubious look. "Xiaoming is a boy's name. Why would your mother be called that?"

A boy's name? Her elegant, imposing stepmother, called by a *boy's* name? Lucy snorted. "I bet you wouldn't say that to her face if she were here," she said under her breath.

"It *isn't* a boy's name," Liao insisted, indignant, "because it's my *mother's* name!" His eyes narrowed. "Take it back."

"Take it back?" Mr. Cerrajero shook his head. "It's a boy's name, and a child's name to boot. I'm not denying your mother could be called that; I'm just saying it's odd." He held up a hand as Liao, his face reddening, opened his mouth to remonstrate. "I've only ever once heard of a girl called Xiaoming, and only in a story about people from thousands of years ago, and that Xiaoming wasn't even real."

"TAKE THAT BACK!" Liao roared. "MY MOTHER IS REAL!"

"He's not talking about your mother, Liao." Lucy pocketed the list of names and dragged her brother away before the argument intensified. Liao, after all, was almost always carrying some sort of explosive. True, he thoroughly objected to using his beloved incendiaries as weapons, but after a perceived insult to his mother ... Well. Better not to take chances. "Thank you for the suggestions, Mr. Cerrajero. *Xièxiè.*"

"Boy's name," Liao muttered scornfully as they departed.

The next pier was more crowded, and there were several craft in the neighborhood of twenty feet moored there. "I wonder which boat we're after," Lucy said, pausing to eye a pretty blue gig outside the tavern.

"How will you know whether it's the right one, when you do find it?" Liao asked. "Apart from it must be big enough for a rocket, if not a gun."

"She'll speak to me the way the *Fate* speaks to me. I shall know, don't worry. Now help me find a spot marked twelve."

"Twelve's yonder," a passing woman interjected, pointing farther down. "Hard by the lens grinder's shop. The sign of the spyglass, you see?"

"Thank you." Lucy took Liao's arm and the two of them threaded through the crowding bodies, trying hard not to bump anyone or to step on the sailors and craftsmen who, like Jianming Cerrajero, lounged against the pilings as they worked. At last they reached the shingle shaped like a telescope and, not far from that, a piling painted with the number 12. The young man leaning against it was busy repairing a snatch block, and his feet rested on the gunwale of a beautiful craft painted a warm dove gray. "Begging pardon," Lucy asked, "but are you Mr. Yarrow?"

The young man looked up from the broken pulley. "Aye?"

She held out her hand. "Compliments, Mr. Yarrow." It was hard to focus on politeness. What she really wanted was to examine the dove-colored launch. At Lucy's best guess, she was around thirty-two feet. Too big, certainly, but she was lovely.

"That's my *Goshawk*," Yarrow replied, returning to his work. "She's not for sale."

Lucy wilted a little. "Mr. Cerrajero on John Agony Pier thought you had a vessel that was."

"Jianming sent you?" At last Yarrow set the block aside. "I might, at that. Who wants to know?"

"I do."

"Be serious."

"I *am* serious! Do you have a boat for sale or no?"

Yarrow gave a low whistle as he got to his feet. "Hear her. This way, Commander." He led Lucy and Liao around the corner of the lens grinder's shop, and there he bent and lifted up on an iron ring to reveal a trapdoor in the pier and a ladder leading down. "She's tied up to the ladder. Have a peep, and welcome."

Liao leaned over the hatchway and peered into the murk. "She's *under the pier?*" He leaned farther, and Lucy grabbed hold of his shirt to keep him from tumbling in.

"Yep. And she's not the only one. It's a place to keep 'em, you see."

Lucy gave Yarrow a long look. She touched the bosun's whistle under her shirt to be sure it was within easy reach, then set her foot on the first rung. "Stay here," she told Liao with a firm shake of her finger.

Her eyes adjusted quickly as she lowered herself down rung by rung. It was shadowy there, but dappled with sunlight that fell onto the surface of the river through chinks between the planks of the pier. A few yards to either side, where there were breaks between the quays, daylight fell full and bright on the water, and in the dark spaces in between, the shapes of boats crouched like sleeping swans with their heads under their wings. Their unstepped masts lay flat along their backs like spines.

"See her, then?" the young man called from above. "Just there, to your left."

"I do," Lucy replied as she clung to the ladder inches above the lapping water and examined the nearest vessel.

Yarrow's boat was a cutter, about sixteen feet from bow to stern and roughly six feet across. It was hard to tell in the gloom, but her hull looked to be a weathered sort of greenish brown. Perhaps she had once been a nice piney green and was in need of a fresh pot of paint, or perhaps she was brown and had been down here so long that she'd collected lichen and needed scraping. Her prow was scuffed badly, probably the result of grinding against the underside of the pier when the river rose. Poor thing.

The vessel seemed so very small; she didn't even have a deck. But, Lucy reminded herself, anything that wasn't a full-size schooner was going to seem small to her. And if the overall effect of Yarrow's cutter was a bit more like an oversize rowboat, at least there was a mast, lying flat along the length of the boat. With that mast in place, she'd be a different craft altogether.

Lucy climbed in and stood quite still with her hand on the port gunwale. At rest, the cutter had very little to say—she needed wind in her sails and water rushing along her sides to speak properly— but she whispered in small creaks and subtle shiftings and the manner in which she listed this way or that with every move Lucy made. And Lucy listened, and imagined.

"How is it?" Liao called from the square of daylight above.

"How is *she*," Lucy corrected absently. "Shhh." She crossed to the starboard side, climbing carefully across the mast, then made her way forward to see what the bow had to say. She leaned over the prow and ran her fingers as far as she could reach down the sharp outer angle that was the most forward edge of the boat. Someone long ago had carved a pattern into the prow. Not a figurehead—small boats like this one didn't get figureheads—but some sort of decoration that had been painted over and over, probably by later owners, until it had become all but invisible. Once upon a time, however, someone had cared enough about this boat to pretty her up.

"Lucy!" Liao called impatiently. "Mayn't I just come down and see?"

"In a minute," she called back. "Just a minute." She wanted a few more moments alone with the cutter without Liao hopping around.

She made her way aft, feeling the motion of the undecked hull underfoot. She knelt and ran her fingers over the seams; she examined the tiller; she winced at the moldering canvas that lay alongside the mast.

This boat would need work, but surely she deserved better than to be left alone here with her mast and this disreputable old sail lying all undone like the broken wing of some great bird. She deserved better than to be ignored, forgotten in the dark, while other vessels came and went on the river.

"Lucy," Liao whined. "May I come and see?"

"No," she called as she climbed back up onto the pier. "Thank you, Mr. Yarrow. We've a few other boats to consider before we decide."

It would never do to fall in love with the very first barky she looked at. But her heart gave a little twinge as she and Liao left Tom Yarrow's green-flanked cutter behind.

❖

In the red stone building that housed the Quenching Press, Trigemine stood on the second-floor gallery outside room number 8 and leaned over the railing to scan the tavern below. Ignis Blister was already down there, waving to him from a table set with a cup of coffee and a bread barge. But the huge, dark figure of Christopher Swifte, the Ironmonger, wasn't present. Trigemine searched the room for the Jumper, but apart from the spectacles and a vague memory of lightish hair, he couldn't remember what the creature had looked like. Which was probably how the Jumper had wanted it.

What did a Jumper want with the Albatross, anyway? Jumpers weren't known for using weapons. If they wanted to get quarrelsome, they could do it all on their own. Or at least they did so in unpredictable ways that didn't involve normal, everyday things like knives.

Trigemine gave a tug on the bell pull that called the lift. It creaked to a stop on the second floor, a giant birdcage on a thick, gutta-percha-coated cable. He climbed inside, rapped on the floor with one heel, and gripped the bars as the lift lurched downward.

"I went ahead and saw to breakfast," Blister said as Trigemine joined him. "And by the by, your Jumper's surname is Coffrett. The tavern keeper doesn't know his Christian name. He arrived a fortnight ago from somewhere out of town."

"Is he staying here?"

"At the Quenching Press? No. Nor did my informant know where to find him. The Ironmonger, by the way, turned up only yesterday, so this Coffrett fellow may have done some sort of computations similar to yours, only not quite as specific."

"And now I'm going to have to redo mine, blast it all."

"And can you? Redo them?"

"I'll have to do an entirely new set, but I always carry a kit with me." Trigemine did not add that he'd brought only the bare minimum of gadgets and that with the complexity of the situation it would take several days to do the sort of reckonings he felt comfortable trusting. "But how did you learn so much so quickly?" he asked, reaching for the bread barge as the server arrived with a second cup.

"I told the tavern keeper I was meant to be meeting a customer. I said I thought I had seen the man last night, but hadn't wanted to interrupt him as he was dining with another fellow. I also figured out, quite by accident, where we might find the source of the powder I've been smelling. The tavern keeper was good enough to recommend that if I had trouble finding my man again, I might find more buyers aboard a ship that arrived recently whose gunner's been buying up massive stores of powder. Evidently the captain owns a great house high on that hill where the firework went up yesterday." Plates of bacon and thin flapjacks arrived. "Privateering ship," Blister added quietly when the server had gone. "A schooner called the *Left-Handed Fate*."

"I meant for you to wait until I came back and *then* we'd see about a boat," Kendrick groused as Lucy led the way to the sign of the telescope.

"Just have a look, will you? We visited four others while you were gone. This one is special. Tell him, Liao!"

"I never saw it," Liao said grouchily. "She hasn't let me see any of them properly, Kendrick."

"What makes her special, Miss Bluecrowne?" the coxswain asked patiently.

Lucy shook her head. "You'll see for yourself." She hoped he would, anyhow. She wasn't certain herself what she'd say if he pressed her for an answer.

Tom Yarrow was right where they'd left him, and after brief introductions were exchanged, he lifted the hatch in the pier again. Lucy did what she could to keep herself from hopping up and down as Kendrick descended into the murk, and as soon as he stepped off the ladder and disappeared, she scrambled down after him. He grinned at her from the stern of the green cutter. "No patience in you, is there, Miss Bluecrowne?"

"What do you think?" she asked, reaching for the gunwale to step in as well.

"Just you give me half a minute before you go asking any questions," he said, making his way forward. "Small for a cutter, but a cutter she is. She's fitted for sweeps and broad enough for two men to row. And will you look at that." He nodded at a bit of ironmongery in the bow, bemused. "I can't quite believe anyone thought she'd carry a gun, but someone thought he might try one in her at some point."

Kendrick crept slowly back to the stern again, examining every inch along the way and giving Lucy forbidding glares whenever she tried to hurry him toward an opinion. At long last, he finished his examination and whistled from the tiller. "Miss Bluecrowne."

She darted aft. "What do you *think*?"

"What makes her special?" he asked again. "She'll need work, you know. I imagine the captain would happily find you something with a bit more polish, like, even if it cost a mint of money."

He likely would, too—he didn't typically spoil Lucy and Liao, but if it meant making life ashore more palatable for her, Lucy suspected he'd not blink at any price, so long as it was a vessel within her sailing capabilities. And yet . . . She chewed on a chapped knuckle.

"What makes her special, Lucy?" Kendrick repeated gently.

How to explain it? "I suppose I have a sort of . . . fellow feeling for her," she admitted in an undertone. The coxswain nodded once, as if this were a perfectly logical answer, but made no reply. "Is she really in such bad condition?" Lucy asked.

"Well, it's worth having her out on the river, at least. But don't go wishing too hard until we've seen her with her mast stepped." He eyed the canvas skeptically. "And that sail . . ."

"But what do you *think*?" Lucy insisted.

The coxswain sighed, but there was a smile lurking around his mouth. "I think—if you insist on an answer I might well be obliged to change once we've had her out on a cruise—I think she could be a right sweet little barky. If the price is right," he added a bit more loudly, "and if she passes muster under sail. And if all this green doesn't turn out to be rot in the sunlight."

"It's old paint," came Yarrow's voice from above, sounding insulted, "and you give me an hour, I'll have her mast stepped and ready for your damned cruise. Come up and get out of my way."

Lucy obeyed and took up a post at the pier's edge, sitting next to Liao. After a brief conference with Kendrick, Yarrow punted the boat from under the pier with a long pole, and as the cutter slid into the light of day, Lucy could see that the patchy green of the old flaked paint was broken here and there by glimmers that might've been even older gold leaf peeking out from underneath. Gold leaf and a carved prow—someone had surely loved this little barky, once upon a time.

Yarrow gave a sharp whistle. Two more sailors came ambling out of nowhere, and the three of them got to work under Kendrick's watchful eye.

"Liao," Lucy said, leaning her elbows on her knees and inspecting every motion of the boat as Kendrick and Yarrow and the tars moved in and about it, "name for me a few sorts of fireworks, would you?"

"What sort of sorts?" Liao asked, busily peeling a splinter away from a plank beside his foot.

"Any sorts. I just want to hear names."

"Oh." He tugged on his queue. "Let's see. There are rockets: sky rockets, towering rockets, caduceus rockets, courantines—"

"Courantine," Lucy repeated experimentally. "Is that French?"

"Yes. It's from that great book of recipes Papa brought for me from London."

Regrettable. "Can't be French, though I do like the word. Go on."

"Well, apart from rockets, there are stars, which are used to ornament more elaborate things: strung stars, trailed stars, driven stars, rolled stars . . ."

"Driven stars?"

"Yes. I use those when I make air balloon fireworks."

"Driven star," she repeated softly.

"Shall I tell you more?"

"If you like, Liao."

He chattered away, listing the names of incendiaries in English and their translations in Chinese and occasionally Latin and Italian as well, but Lucy only half listened.

In the cutter, Yarrow took something from his pocket and bent down with it in his hand as his two mates began levering the mast upward. "A coin, probably," Lucy explained to Liao. "The old tars say one always ought to tuck a coin under the mast, in case the ship finds itself crossing the River Styx and needing to pay the Devil's ferryman." Lucy saw Kendrick remove his hand from his own pocket. Likely he'd had a coin ready in the event that Yarrow forgot.

"Excellent," Liao said with relish.

At last the single yard climbed the mast and the patched sail rose and shivered in the breeze, and the cutter was ready. "Come along," Lucy said, hauling Liao to his feet. "Step lively."

She had thought anything with a single mast would look disappointingly like a child's sailboat, but this one decidedly did not. Most toy sailboats had a triangular fore-and-aft-rigged sail, but the cutter had a square sail that hung from a yard high up on the mast: a dipping lug-sail, which would allow her to change course swiftly and efficiently across the wind.

"In you come, miss," Yarrow said, steadying the boat for her and Liao. "I hear your father's the master of the handsome schooner up at James Ordeal Pier. Supposing we take the boat there and back? That ought to give you a sense of her."

"Has she a name?" Lucy asked as he cast off.

"Sure she did once, but I never knew it." He winked. "You'll have to come up with one."

"*If* we buy her," Kendrick cautioned Lucy from the stern. "Not before. Give her a name and you won't want to give her back."

"Understood," Lucy said obediently. She put her hands on the gunwale again as the cutter slid gracefully out into the river. Now the boat would certainly have something to say. Perhaps she might even whisper her name, if Lucy listened hard enough. Or perhaps she already had.

"Miss Bluecrowne," Kendrick called, "should you like to take the tiller?"

In the shadow of a countinghouse, Blister stopped and extended an ash-stained finger. "That's the ship."

It was moored at the end of the pier. Trigemine gave the vessel a cursory glance, but not knowing—or caring—much at all about seagoing things, he didn't have any particular opinion about it. He also couldn't smell the bizarre powder aroma that Blister had followed there like a hound tracking a fox. "That's the one?"

"Oh, yes." Blister sniffed the air for the fiftieth time. "What an odd, wonderful combination. Some of these chemicals I have never encountered outside my own compounds. Why on earth would a privateer carry them? They hardly recommend themselves for gunnery. And yet it's probably the gunner we're after, or one of his mates."

"And so . . . ?"

"Well, fortunately, they're in the market for powder, which means it ought to be easy enough to—" Blister broke off speaking and whipped his head around to squint at a small sailboat heading for the ship. He inhaled the breeze carrying the boat toward them, frowned, breathed again, and fumbled for his scissors-glasses. "Unless . . ."

"Unless what?" The little boat was slicing rapidly through the water, and now it was close enough for Trigemine to make out four figures within: two men and two children. One was a boy who was perched up front like a figurehead. The one who appeared to be steering, despite wearing her hair short-cropped, was almost certainly a girl.

"Unless I'm wrong," Blister answered slowly, lowering the glasses. "Unless it's that boy."

"The *boy?*"

"Indeed."

Now the craft was close enough for Trigemine to see the children's faces. The girl was blond and tanned, but plainly of European heritage. The boy, dark-haired and wearing a long, thin braid, was not. "What makes you think it's the boy?"

Blister observed the children closely as they hailed the ship from their respective seats. "I suspect the boy is Chinese. The chemicals I smell coming off the ship . . . Well, the names would mean nothing to you, but they are uncommon ingredients on the Atlantic. When I've had them, I've gotten them from fellows in the Canton trade. And nearly every formula I've ever seen that calls for them has derived in some fashion from Chinese alchemy." He tapped one of the silver-framed lenses against his chin. "This is very interesting."

"This is problematic." There were different logistics to consider if their mark was a child. Different likelihoods. Different probabilities.

"Well, if nothing else, carrying a child back to Morvengarde will be easier than carrying an adult, if he isn't inclined to come willingly." Blister smiled, and it was a cunning smile, a cold smile. "And children love fireworks."

SIX

THE *DRIVEN STAR*

DESPITE Kendrick's warnings, by the time she laid the cutter along the freshly painted emerald side of the *Left-Handed Fate,* Lucy was already in love. The threadbare, patched sail had caught the breeze easily though it really shouldn't have, and the tiller had sung in Lucy's palm, eagerly answering every request she'd made. It was as if the boat had been longing for a cruise, longing for a friend. Oh, the two of them were going to get on just fine.

"Run up and see if Chips can spare a moment," Kendrick said, fending the boat off the new paintwork. "And then you might go and ask Mr. Santat and Mr. Burrows if we've got any spare number-five canvas. I don't know as you'll be able to convince Sails to make it himself, not unless he's got nothing else in the world to do, but the raw stuff for a new sail we ought to be able to manage."

Breathless, Lucy left the others in the cutter and used one of the *Fate*'s lines to pull herself rapidly up the side of the schooner and onto the deck. Immediately, her excitement about the little boat below was drowned in a wave of homesickness for this vessel and her comfortable, familiar place aboard it. She resisted the urge to run straight to the bow to lean out and touch the furled wing of the blindfolded figurehead, a woman who was as much a part of her family as any member of the crew and whose upraised left hand had always seemed to Lucy to be lifted in welcome. Greeting the figurehead was part of Lucy's coming-aboard ritual, but today she knew it might just break her heart in two.

The deck would've looked like chaos to anyone who wasn't familiar with the workings of a ship of war, but to Lucy's eye the motion on deck was perfectly organized, something very like a dance. Here Mr. Burrows and his mates were busy at work; over there the gunner was supervising the shipping of a new number four gun to replace the one that had broken its moorings and smashed its way overboard in a recent engagement with a French brig. Mr. Foster, the second mate, and Mr. Santat, the purser, who managed the *Fate*'s accounts and provisions, were deep in conversation with a man Lucy didn't know, likely a merchant from the Harbors who'd come aboard by the gangplank between the *Fate* and the pier on the larboard side. Overhead, the rigging was crawling with busy tars, and from the open hatches voices told of more hands laboring below under the keen eye of Mr. Fitch, the first mate, who would be seeing to the restowing of the hold. Amid all the bustle, a trio of lucky off-watch sailors dressed in their fanciest shore-going rigs sauntered down the gangplank. Lucy didn't have to see the deck of cards in each man's pocket to know they were probably heading out on a traditional Nagspeake pilgrimage, in which sailors went around to churches dedicated to the saints who looked after seafarers, leaving a prayer card at each one until they'd visited the lot.

Lucy blinked away a sudden stinging in her eyes and turned to salute the quarterdeck as proper manners required. She returned the salutes of a few of her shipmates—her *former* shipmates, she thought sadly—then she blinked some more and went in search of the carpenter.

She found him slung over the larboard side near the bow, examining a spot where one of the French brig's shots had hit. The only remaining sign of the damage was the unpainted patch, and several sailors with pots of paint waited impatiently to finish the work.

At last the carpenter nodded and hauled himself back up onto the deck. "My compliments, Mr. Raines, and have you got a minute to look at a boat?" Lucy inquired.

Mr. Raines paused in his salute. "Is it that blasted cutter again? Begging your pardon, miss, and it's nice to see you back aboard."

"Not the cutter. Well, not the *Fate*'s cutter. A cutter for me," Lucy said, restraining herself from tugging at his sleeve. "Kendrick has her tied up to starboard."

"Is that so? I imagine I have a moment or two for that." He turned and whistled sharply. "Pass the word for Mr. Prim." Mr. Prim was the bosun, who managed the deck and the rigging.

A few minutes later, Lucy and Liao were leaning over the starboard rail, surveying the scene in the cutter below as the carpenter went over every inch of timber and the bosun examined the mast and yard and both of them shouted up to the purser, who stood at the railing with an inkhorn in his buttonhole and a notebook in one hand. One of the sailmaker's mates waited nearby, and Lucy had the very strong impression that the moment a decision was reached, not only would he rouse out a spare bolt of canvas, but he'd find his own duties magically re-allocated elsewhere and nothing better to do with his time than to begin making a fresh new sail.

"Thank goodness there's no actual work to be done on this schooner." Lucy glanced up guiltily to see her father standing at her side, amused. "It seems everyone's found something he'd rather be doing than refitting the *Fate*. As you were," he barked at the shame-faced seamen within earshot. "How's she look, then, Mr. Raincs?"

Everyone in the cutter looked up and saluted. "Not bad nor half, sir," the carpenter replied. "A bit rough, but one day's work and I'd trust her on the open sea."

"There's nothing wrong with her that needs even half a day's work," Yarrow argued.

"Well, that'd be to put her right Navy fashion, of course," Mr. Raines said airily. "We like things done Navy fashion when possible."

"She wants a new yard, too, begging your pardon," the bosun added. "Mr. Raines could cut down one of them old spars we switched out. And of course, you see the state of her canvas."

Yarrow groused a bit more, but certainly he knew the Fates wouldn't have wasted time poking and prodding and talking about the work they'd like to do if they didn't think it was a boat worth putting that work into.

Lucy's father leaned close. "Should you like to have this boat, Lucy?"

"Yes, please, sir," Lucy whispered.

"Very good." Captain Bluecrowne called the purser over. "Mr. Santat, would you be so kind as to see to the details?"

The cutter was hers, or would be quite soon. She squeezed her father's hand and reminded herself to hug Kendrick very, very hard as soon as he came up.

"You have your work cut out for you," Captain Bluecrowne said, squeezing back. "I'll give you whatever supplies you need, but what can be done by your own two hands you must do yourself. You can't say fairer than that."

Lucy saluted eagerly. "Aye aye, sir!"

Just at that moment, the ship's bell tolled eight times, and the beautiful order on the deck dissolved immediately as the hands were piped to dinner. The men in the cutter returned. "One cutter, purchased," the purser said.

"My thanks, Mr. Santat," Lucy said. "And Papa." As an afterthought, she leaned over the gunwale and searched for the departing Yarrow on the pier. "My thanks, Mr. Yarrow! I'll take good care of her, sir!"

Yarrow looked up and waved. "I know you will, miss. Give you joy of her!"

Lucy turned back to her father imploringly. "May I begin today?"

"Start your work tomorrow," Captain Bluecrowne said severely, sharing the order out equally among Lucy, the bosun, the carpenter, and the sailmaker's mate, who were lurking nearby. "And make sure Mr. Fitch approves every hand who offers to help. He shan't be happy with any of us if we damage his schedule."

Lucy saluted. "Tomorrow it is, sir. May we run her back to the house?"

He glanced from one sailor to the next. "What say you? Do we trust the barky that far in her current state?" The little group mumbled variously about last looks-over and how they'd have better answers in a few hours. Captain Bluecrowne shook his head, not fooled at all. "Did you not just hear me say Lucy's to do the work herself?"

All three cast reproachful glances at him and Lucy tried not to grin. "Best respects, sir," the carpenter began, "but—"

The captain sighed. Then he kissed Lucy's forehead and ruffled Liao's hair. "It appears that you may be able to sail her back after a more thorough *inspection* has been done. Should you both like to have dinner with me at four bells?"

"Will there be ship's biscuit?" Liao asked hopefully. "The crunchy sort? There doesn't seem to be much crunchy ship's biscuit when we're in port."

Nobody aboard could figure out how Liao had gotten the idea that hardtack was some sort of seagoing delicacy instead of just stale biscuit. He even managed to be entertained by the way weevils fell out of it when one knocked it against the table. Still, "I shall make sure of it," Captain Bluecrowne promised.

"The ship ahoy!" On the pier, a small man in a long velvet coat stood waving with wild cheer. Behind him a bigger man with a tall hat perched on his head and piercing blue eyes stood with arms folded.

"Those'll be the powder merchants," the purser said. "Pass the word for Mr. Harrick."

"Powder merchants?" Liao murmured, craning his neck over the gunwale with interest.

A moment later a sailor came jogging back, his bare feet slapping on the deck. "Mr. Harrick's compliments, but he can't be interrupted just now, and would the gents come back at six bells in the afternoon watch?"

Lucy was only half paying attention to this exchange. There was something strange about the taller man. Maybe it was the eyes. His blue gaze was discomfiting. It bordered on cold, although the rest of his face was open and he was even smiling a bit at his colleague's childlike excitement.

The purser relayed the gunner's request, and the two merchants assented. Then they were gone.

"Well, miss?"

Lucy turned and flung her arms around Kendrick's waist. "Thank you."

He patted her back. "What's her name, then? Because I know perfectly well you've had one in mind since before we left Yarrow's wharf."

She blushed. "So I have." Together they leaned over the gunwale and contemplated Lucy's first command. "She's the *Driven Star*."

Trigemine took his watch from his trouser pocket and thumbed it open. "I presume you know what's meant by 'six bells.' I don't."

Blister's jovial demeanor melted away, leaving his eyes unnaturally sharp. "Three-thirty. But it hardly matters. It's neither the gunner nor any of his mates we need. It's the boy."

"You're certain?"

"I am. The boy is our conflagrationeer." Blister scratched his head, then smoothed his hair down again as they walked along the wharf toward the shore. "I suppose, with your knife business unresolved, we can't just grab him and use the kairos mechanism to hop away?"

"Just so. Hence my words yesterday about not wanting to behave like a press gang. Ordinarily, there would be no difficulty at all."

"I wonder how he came by his gifts." Blister sounded troubled. "Learned from the gunner, perhaps? That's not uncommon . . . but how did he come to be aboard a British ship to begin with? And the usual stores of a British powder magazine would not account for those rare ingredients."

"What does it matter?"

"It matters because— Well, perhaps I'm wrong. Perhaps it doesn't matter, particularly if it comes to a grab in the end. And it likely will," Blister warned. He glanced over his shoulder and raised the scissors-glasses to his eyes as he peered back at the schooner.

"It would have to be a child, wouldn't it?" This was going to take some figuring.

"Doesn't that make it easier?" Blister replied with a singular lack of concern.

Trigemine sighed. "It's easier in many ways, but apart from the unfortunate matter of whatever adults we shall have to separate him from, children are not natural roamers. There are exceptions, of course, but I don't imagine we can simply convince him to come over to our way of life and into Morvengarde's employ. To say nothing of the employ of the man who ordered up the conflagrationeer from Morvengarde," he added grimly.

Blister looked at him. "You know who the buyer is?"

"I do, though I don't believe I was meant to know, and I rather wish I didn't."

"But you work for *Morven arde*," Blister said doubtfully. "You work for the most frightening man I've ever met in the flesh, and I'm older than the hills."

"You work for him too, at the moment."

"But my point is—"

"I take your point just fine, Blister." Trigemine removed his hat and rubbed his forehead. "I'm afraid of Morvengarde. I'd be a fool not to be, and you'd know me for a liar if I didn't admit it. But Morvengarde is neither the only nor the most frightening being of his kind on the roads." He gave Blister a meaningful stare and waited for the peddler to figure it out.

Blister thought for a moment. Then the color drained from his face. "Oh."

"Now you take *my* point."

"I'm—I'm working for—" He took a step backward and felt for the nearest piling. "Am I—?"

Since Blister didn't seem to be able to say the name himself, Trigemine said it for him. "Jack Hellcoal. Yes."

"Jack Hellcoal." Now the peddler's voice had an audible tremor to it. Trigemine couldn't blame him. "I've heard at least five stories about who he really is. Where he came from, how he got his name . . ."

"I figure we all have."

"Do you know? The truth, I mean?"

"I didn't get any special insight from Morvengarde, if that's what you're asking."

"I always liked the one about how he beat the Devil," Blister said. "Now, that's a story to have told about yourself! Turned away at the gates of Heaven, refused at the gates of Perdition, all on account of you bested the Devil and even *he* didn't want to see your face again. What a tale! 'Take this coal and start your own Hell.' From the Devil himself!"

"Unless."

"Yes." The peddler licked his lips. "Unless, of course, it's true and I'm working for him. In which case I do not like that story so much."

"I don't know if that particular one's accurate," Trigemine cautioned. "I've also heard he won the coal from another roamer in a game of chance. I've heard it came from the Devil, but that Jack hadn't ever met him before that moment. I've heard there are three, and *only* three, roamers who know the truth for sure, and all three are stark raving mad. But I *can* tell you that Jack does, in fact, have a bit of infernal coal, because Morvengarde's price for finding a conflagrationeer was a piece of that coal, and Morvengarde would have insisted on seeing it."

"Have you . . . *you* haven't met him, have you?" Blister asked.

"Jack?" Trigemine glanced sideways at the peddler. "Yourself?" he asked casually.

"Never," Blister replied promptly.

"At least not yet," Trigemine said slowly.

"Yes, I suppose, if you want to be pedantic about it. So, have you?"

"Let's just say, I've been in the same room with him," Trigemine said cautiously. "I wouldn't say we'd *met.*" *Thank the stars,* he added silently.

"And?" Blister asked explosively when Trigemine didn't elaborate.

"And? And what?"

"And what *happened* when you were in the same room?" Blister demanded. "All those stories—tell me something you know to be true. Even if it's just what kind of liquor the man drinks."

"The only time I saw him drink, it was water," Trigemine said, still thinking. Beginning to calculate. Because there was something about the time he'd met Jack that had always confused him. A thing Jack had known that he shouldn't have—except, improbably, for the intervention of this very man now standing before him, looking impatient. Ignis Blister, although he had never—yet—met

Jack Hellcoal, would one day surface to offer Jack an impossible piece of information that *he*, Blister, should also never have had.

How had he gotten that information? Trigemine had always wondered. But now he saw an unexpected answer to that question. It seemed too simple, and yet sometimes the most elegant mathematics were the simplest.

Blister glared at him. "Will you please stop doing whatever you're doing and—"

Trigemine held up a finger. He glanced down the pier, spotted the clustering tables of a tavern, and crooked a finger. When they were seated and had ordered drinks, he folded his hands. "The story I'm going to tell now," he said slowly, "involves you."

The blood drained from Blister's face. "Me?"

Trigemine nodded once. "'Start your own Hell,' the Devil supposedly said to Jack, but a fellow can't create his own Hell out of nothing but a piece of infernal coal. Jack's got to find an existing place of power and claim it for his own. I saw him do something in preparation for one such attempt that I think says something about the sort of man he is. This happened—happens—ten years or so from now."

"Is this related to why he wants his own conflagrationeer?" Blister worried his chin with nervous fingers. "He'd need someone to take the coal and start the fire with which one can claim a city."

Trigemine inclined his head. "A conflagrationeer can provide the right fire, but, of course, fire is only part of the process. A city is claimed by fire, by naming, and by blood. Now, there are several ways to carry out the blood claiming—in fact, one of them involves the use of a blade with certain properties we believe the Albatross—the knife Morvengarde wants from the Ironmonger—to have. Another way involves toppling the pillars of the city and installing new ones."

"Pillars?"

"A community has folks who are like pillars—they hold it together and shape its character. There's almost always a smith, a keeper of lore, and a keeper of sanctuary, and then the others can vary. A fellow like Jack would need to either turn those pillars to his side or topple them. And by *topple*, obviously, I mean *kill*. That could fulfill the blood requirement."

"A smith?" Blister's eyebrows rose. "Didn't the Jumper say something to the Ironmonger about a crossroads town needing a blacksmith?"

Trigemine nodded significantly. "And," he added darkly, "if he knew we'd overheard that, our Jumper would be none too happy about it. The more powerful the crossroads, the more powerful the group, and the more likely they are to keep their roles a secret. Because of the probability of someone like Jack. The world may never have seen precisely his ilk before, but the world has surely always been aware of the odds of someone like him turning up on the roads eventually. Which brings us back to the man himself."

Trigemine paused as a server deposited two mugs on the table and disappeared again. "In about ten years, in a small town, a couple hundred miles down the coast from here, Jack goes right up to the keeper of lore—which on its own is strange, because, again, these people tend to keep a pretty low profile—and asks him to tell a particular tale, an anecdote from the town's past. An innocuous one, to all appearances—even to the keeper of lore, it's not clear why Jack should care. But he recognized *Jack,* so he also knows that whatever Jack's asking, he should probably say no . . . and he does. At which point, Jack offers to bet him for the story."

Blister coughed on a mouthful of beer. "And the keeper of lore *takes* that bet?"

"Yes. Because of Jack's collateral. You see, at the edge of town there's a very, very old, long-abandoned orchard, and there were— are . . . creatures in it. The denizens of the town and the denizens of the grove have lived in a sort of uneasy peace for about a hundred years, but in the months leading up to Jack's arrival, that begins to change. Parts of the street start sinking where things tunnel under them. Peculiar shadows slide through the alleys at night. People go missing. People turn up again, but not in the same condition. And what Jack knows, which I've never been able to figure out, because even the keeper of lore himself—a man who carries the collective memory of the town within him—doesn't know it, is that the creatures in the grove can be bound by salt."

Blister gave him a skeptical look. "Half the uncanny things in the world can be bound by salt."

"These things require salt of copper," Trigemine said. "And

Jack and his men happen to have four saddlebags full of it, which they bought on a tip from *you*, Blister. Somehow, in that future time, you know what even the townsfolk do not—that these creatures are vulnerable to the stuff. Speaking to the keeper, Jack calls it blue vitriol."

"Yes, that's copper salt." Blister frowned, confused. "It has a dozen uses in fireworking, but I've never heard of it used to . . ." He paused, then looked up sharply. "You can kill certain parasites with it. Certain plants, certain pests . . . fungus . . . Are these things in some way . . . how would you even . . . are they *horticultural?*"

Trigemine grinned and lifted his mug. "There it is."

"And they buy it from *me?*" Blister stared. "But I don't know anything about—I've never even *heard* of . . . how could I possibly . . ."

"I suspect you'll know to tell Jack *then*," Trigemine explained, "because *I'm* telling you *now*. But if we get hung up on time paradoxes, we'll never get to the point, which is that Jack and the keeper of lore agree to the bet. The stakes are that if Jack wins, the keeper will give him the story he wants, and if Jack loses, he'll take the stockpile of blue vitriol that he and his men *just happen* to have with them and contain the creatures that are menacing the town.

"The participants agree that Jack is allowed to pick the specific wager, and he chooses a horse race; the keeper is permitted to add one additional term, and he declares that he and Jack will bet on each other's proxies to win. Wisely, he lays the condition at the very last minute before the gunshot signals the start, so that, under the terms of the wager, when Jack's rider wins—surprising no one who sees the man and his horse—the keeper of lore wins the bet. So Jack shakes his hand and prepares to fulfill the terms of his loss."

Trigemine took a long drink. "That night he and his men take their stockpile of blue vitriol and use it not to kill the creatures, but to drive them straight out of the trees and *into the town*. Jack sets fire to a fuse and traps them there inside a ring of burning vitriol. And then, having technically fulfilled his obligation—he's contained the things, after all—Jack walks right through the fire and up to the keeper of lore, who's hiding with his neighbors in the saloon, and demands his tale. He gets it, of course. Then he asks for a glass of water—gets that, too. When he's drunk it down, he leaves the saloon without another word and walks right back through town and through the fire and out again, leaving the place to its fate."

"He doesn't—he just leaves them all there?" Blister asked, aghast. "He doesn't keep his end of the bargain and, well, save them?"

"Aha, but that time there *is* no bargain. In the panic of the moment, the keeper assumes that he and the town are hostages, and if he gives Jack what he wants, Jack will undo what he's done. But the keeper doesn't—didn't set the condition." Trigemine shrugged. "He should've known better."

"Is that . . . is that where he finally does it?" Blister asked, lowering his voice to a whisper. "Creates his own Hell?"

Trigemine shook his head slowly. "Turns out the keeper's tale is actually the key to an attempt on a wholly different city. Jack sacrifices an entire town for a story."

"And you saw this?"

"I happened to be passing through." Trigemine finished his beer. "I was in the saloon at the end. I didn't stick around to see how it played out, as you can imagine." He touched his watch pocket. "Picked a better moment and hopped to it with the utmost dispatch."

"Jack Hellcoal," Blister repeated, drawing a hand down his chin. His fingers weren't quite steady. Once again, Trigemine could sympathize. He knew what had to be running through Blister's mind right now: *Does he know I'm working for him? Will he come after me if anything goes wrong? Will Morvengarde throw me to the wolves if I fail?* Questions Trigemine had often wondered himself on previous jobs when he'd been sent out on behalf of other Morvengarde clients. But Trigemine had been doing this a long time, and he was too valuable for Morvengarde to cast off so easily, even if this deal went wrong.

But. *But.* This particular client was not like any other. Certainly Morvengarde would have made much of the fact that he'd put Trigemine, his best sutler, on the task, and had arranged to bring aboard the very best contractor to ensure that what the sutler brought back was exactly what Jack had paid for. So yes, Trigemine figured Jack would know it was he and Blister who'd fouled up if anything went wrong. Morvengarde would take the blame—he was too good a man of business to do otherwise—but there was no one to step fully into the Great Merchant's shoes if anything happened to him. He'd survive Jack's fury.

No, if they failed and Jack Hellcoal decided to hand down some retribution, maybe to send a message warning the rest of the roaming world against making mistakes on his time, he'd go after Trigemine and Blister. Losing Trigemine would damage Morvengarde's business enough to punish him plenty. And if Jack hunted down Blister, one of the legendary Yankee Peddlers and a man who'd walked nearly as long as anyone on the roads . . . that would be a message no one in the roaming world could ignore, even if it meant down the line he wouldn't have Blister to tell him about blue vitriol. Jack Hellcoal would undoubtedly manage to find another way to get what he wanted.

Trigemine, of course, had already worked through these possibilities. Blister was doing it now, and while his peddler's poker face was pretty good, it wasn't quite equal to the task at hand.

"Let it be a lesson." Trigemine clapped Blister on the shoulder. "Next time, ask."

The peddler nodded, still a bit thunderstruck. "What on earth does Morvengarde want a piece of hellcoal for?"

Trigemine snorted. "He's the Great Merchant. Why *wouldn't* he want a piece?"

"You mentioned knives for blood claiming. Is the Albatross for Jack Hellcoal too?"

"Not as far as Jack knows. But I suspect Morvengarde will offer it to him as soon as we have it. And I suspect Jack will bargain."

Blister made a thoughtful face. "It occurs to me that if Morvengarde had both a piece of hellcoal and the Albatross, he could think about starting his own Hell too."

"Yes," Trigemine said deliberately. "Yes, he certainly could, if he wanted."

The peddler's eyes narrowed. Then he rearranged his face into something open and guileless. Trigemine followed his gaze. The little boy and the short-haired girl were trotting down the gangplank and onto the wharf.

SEVEN

THE CONFLAGRATIONEER

LUCY had tried to climb down into the *Driven Star* to help with whatever Mr. Raines was up to, but the carpenter had chased her off, insisting that he was merely inspecting the cutter and wouldn't even start at that until after his own meal. So she and Liao had decided to explore a bit more of the Quayside Harbors, the better to kill time until dinner and keep Lucy from driving herself out of her mind with impatience. It wasn't working terribly well.

They were wandering among the shops that crowded the pier when a sudden flash of light blazed from a table outside a tavern. Liao stopped in his tracks, enthralled by the little flare. It was a beautiful shade of azure, and it burned in the palm of the shorter of the two powder merchants who'd hailed the *Fate*.

"Oh," Liao said softly. "Lucy, Lucy, *look*."

She blinked, not sure what she was supposed to be seeing. The two men appeared to be perfectly ordinary coves having pints—perfectly ordinary, except for that flame. It sat in the hollow of the one fellow's hand, a sparking, crackling lick of fire the size of Lucy's thumb. There was no bit of match or tinder to be seen, and stranger still, it didn't seem to be burning the man at all. Although Lucy wasn't always able to share Liao's enthusiasm for fiery things, she had to admit that this strange, minute flame was eerily lovely.

Liao was already edging toward the table for a closer glimpse and waiting for one of the merchants to notice him. In a moment he stood right between the two men with his fingers clasped behind his back, trying to appear polite despite the obvious intrusion he was about to commit.

"Liao, don't interrupt—"

The two merchants looked up from the flame, and the shorter man's hand closed sharply on it. "Hello," he said, eyeing Liao curiously.

"I beg your pardon," Lucy apologized.

"Hello," Liao replied as she grabbed him by the elbow to try to drag him away. "I saw your fire, before."

The merchant had folded his hands together tightly. Now he opened them and held up his palms. "I'm not certain what you mean, my dear lad." But there was something in both his voice and the gesture itself that was irresistibly like a magician demonstrating that there was nothing to be seen just before the proper trick begins. Lucy found that she had let go of Liao and that both of them were leaning toward the table in expectation.

She wiped the anticipation off her face. "Excuse my brother for the interruption. Liao," she hissed. "Come away. Don't be rude."

But then the blue-eyed man spoke up. "Go on, Blister, don't keep the child in suspense. You were a boy once. Anyhow, he caught you fair and square. Don't torture him."

The shorter merchant gave an exaggerated sigh. Then he lifted his spectacles to his eyes and examined Liao as if he were trying to decide something. "This is a secret of my trade," he said severely. "Can you keep a secret?"

"He certainly can't possibly keep it any worse than you already do," the other pointed out. "If you don't want people to see, don't do tricks in public."

"Is it a trick?" Liao asked, disappointed. "A magic trick, like? Then it isn't real?"

The man called Blister looked affronted. "Not real? Young man, I am an *artificier,* not a magician. Yes, I can create illusions, but the fires that make them up are quite real, I assure you." And without taking his eyes from Liao, he rubbed his fingers against his palm for a moment as if he were working loose something sticky. Then he snapped his thumb and middle finger together and flung his hand out, flat. There, right at the middle of the line crossing the center of his palm, was a violet spark. As they watched, the spark kindled itself into a flitting tongue of fire shading from the color of a pale sky to deep cobalt.

Liao leaned across the table, so close to the flicker that his nose reflected a slight blue tone. "It doesn't burn?"

"Oh, it burns, but it doesn't burn hot." The merchant tilted his hand down and the flame slid along the groove between his middle and fourth fingers. He moved his fingertips one after the other in a wave, and the flame slipped easily from each to the next. "It's kindled of a very special compound."

Liao frowned. "There wasn't anything in your hand."

"You didn't *see* anything in my hand," Blister corrected. "That's because the compound is near invisible to the eye. Fire can't come from nothing. It needs —"

"Something for fuel and something to oxidize it," Liao said impatiently. "What's in the compound?"

"Very good," the merchant replied, beaming. "You know something about incendiaries?"

"Yes. What's in the compound?"

"Some ordinary things, and some you won't have heard of."

"But maybe I have!"

Blister appraised Liao again. "They are often called red salt and hard snow," he said with the air of a man giving a test.

"Hard snow?" Lucy repeated. "Meaning ice?"

"No, I know what those are," Liao said immediately. "We call them *chìyán* and *génxuě*, but I've never heard anyone else mention them. Never outside my mother's village back home. There, they are used mostly for a type of *dān*. A sort of medicine, I suppose you would say."

"And 'there' would be China?" Blister asked. Liao nodded. "I thought as much. I learned of them from a Chinese fireworker I met once on a long-ago time." He extended the flame dancing upon his fingers toward Liao. "Should you like to have a closer look? Hold out your hand."

Lucy held her breath as Liao obeyed and the merchant tipped the flame into her brother's open palm. He sucked in a breath, but he didn't flinch, and the little fire went right on flickering just above the surface of his skin.

"Does it hurt?" she asked.

Liao tilted his head. "I can just barely feel when it moves. It feels—it feels like a feather, if a feather were just a bit heavier. What is it called?" he asked, his eyes full of wonder and the glow of the impossible flame he held.

"Cald-fire," Blister said, sounding triumphant. "There are other ways to compound it, mind. I didn't invent it. Just this way of kindling it."

"Cald-fire," Liao repeated.

"You mustn't hold it for too long," the merchant warned. "It does burn, in its way. It will begin to blister you eventually, although you wouldn't feel it straight off."

"Here, Lucy," Liao said eagerly. "Try it!"

Blister shook his head. "No, you'd best call it done, just to be safe. Close your hand now and smother it."

Reluctantly Liao did as he was told, curling his little fingers over the flame. He peeked into his fist as if he'd captured a firefly and wanted to be sure it was still there, then opened his fingers again and stared at his empty hand.

"Very brave," Blister said. "You're not afraid of fire."

"But I know to respect it," Liao said dutifully. Lucy had heard the gunner lecture him on this point many times.

The man with the blue eyes spoke up again. "Very well said." He drained his mug and took a watch from his pocket. "Apologies, Blister, but we'd best get on our way."

"Ah." The other merchant sighed. "Right as always, Trigemine." He finished off his own pint and rose. "Though it has been lovely chatting with such a clever young man. Mostly all we do is talk about boring gunpowder to gunners who only care that we sell it in barrels that won't leak. This has been quite a nice change." He offered his hand to Liao. "My name is Ignis Jonathan Blister."

"Liao Owen Bluecrowne," Liao said after a pause, probably to be sure he put his names in what passed for the right order in this part of the world. "Thank you for showing me the cald-fire, Mr. Blister."

They shook hands solemnly. The other merchant got to his feet and the two of them headed for shore. Liao watched their backs, and Lucy watched Liao.

She'd gotten a cutter. Liao deserved something special too.

Lucy ducked around him and scurried after the departing men. "Mr. Blister, there!"

He turned. "Yes, miss?"

"Do you sell any of the rare ingredients you mentioned? My brother has a workshop of his own, you know. He would use them properly, I'm certain."

"I do have a number of quite uncommon things floating around the wagon at the moment. Ordinarily I don't part with them, no." Blister considered Liao, who was just now catching up. "But today . . . today I just might do. I just might."

Liao held himself very still, plainly not daring to get his hopes up and afraid to so much as breathe while Blister was making his decision.

At last, the merchant's face broke into a broad smile. "Why on earth not? Come along, little firebug, and we shall see what catches your fancy."

✦

The wagon had been left in a clearing near the red stone Quenching Press building. Blister led the way with Liao at his side. The two of them spent the entire walk in rapid, nonstop colloquy, and as far as Trigemine was concerned, they might as well have been speaking a language all their own. He recognized some of the words flying back and forth but had no idea what they were meant to convey: *evolute* and *involute curves, driven stars,* things that sounded like they were being pronounced with capital letters, like *the Mysterious* and *the Yellow.* Other words—*saucissons, gerbes, courantines*—meant nothing at all to him. Liao went on about muds followed by strings of numbers. Blister mentioned something called realgar and Liao delightedly explained that where he came from the same thing was called "stone within the head of the great one's decade."

Trigemine followed slowly, leaving them to their bizarre conversation. The English girl who had called Liao her brother and who had finally introduced herself as Lucy Bluecrowne walked awkwardly somewhere in the middle. There was a sort of sadness about her, but despite that, it was clear that she and Liao were relatively happy children, and that they were devoted to each other.

Happy children didn't kidnap as easily as unhappy ones, who could be lured away with the promise of something better than they thought they had. Worse, Trigemine was beginning to suspect that it was going to be difficult to separate the two of them. Which meant it might come to taking Lucy, too. Or at least putting her out of the way.

If it did come to that, Trigemine would have to handle things. Unless he was very much mistaken, there was no way Blister was going to be up to proper violence. Which wasn't a problem, just something that had to be factored in. There wasn't room for loose ends or slip-ups in this endeavor.

Then there was the matter of Christopher Swifte and the Albatross. And where was the Jumper, meantime, and what was he up to? Did he know about Trigemine?

The girl, Lucy, glanced thoughtfully back at him. He smiled and pitched his voice to a sweet tone. "Are you interested in fireworks as well, then?"

She returned the smile, but there was restraint behind it. "I like them as much as most, I suppose. But I might be closer to the gunners Mr. Blister thinks are boring. I grew up aboard that schooner. It belongs to my father."

"A privateer, are you?"

"We prefer *letter-of-marque*," she said, a little coldly.

"I apologize."

"That's all right."

They continued to walk in silence, half listening to the other two as they prated on, until they arrived at the clearing. Blister and Liao darted ahead to the wagon and hopped up the stairs as if they were a pair of boys on holiday. As Trigemine and Lucy crossed the clearing at a more leisurely pace, the girl spoke up again. "You aren't interested in fireworks either, are you?"

Trigemine glanced sharply at her. "It's that clear, is it?" She lifted her shoulders. "Well, you're not wrong. I confess I know very little about Blister's work, other than if one puts fire to gunpowder it explodes. But someone has to mind the business end of things." He waved a hand to Lucy as they reached the wagon. "Please. After you."

Just then something inside the wagon exploded. A pair of maniacal laughs drifted out along with a puff of red-tinged smoke.

"I'll wait here." Lucy found a stump a few yards off and sat.

Trigemine waved smoke from his face. "Probably wise." He took a cigar from his vest pocket and wandered a short distance away. With an eye on Lucy and an ear cocked toward the wagon, he bit off one end of the cigar and lit the other. He let his thoughts wander back to the problem of the Ironmonger and the Jumper as he smoked.

It isn't a question of beating his offer. It's a question of whether I want to deal with him. Or, I suppose now, whether I want to deal with you.

A short while later, the wagon door opened and Blister and the boy came rushing down the steps, each with an armful of infernal devices. They deposited their booty on the ground and began to divide it into piles, resembling nothing so much as a pair of manic children sorting gifts at Christmas. "Here it is," Blister said, examining through his glasses a lumpy ball wrapped in bright blue marbled paper with a length of fuse hanging from it.

Liao barely managed to wait until Blister held the ball out before snatching it from his hand. He dashed to Lucy and waved the ball under her nose. "Lucy, look! Come and see what I made!"

"Shall we try it, Liao?" Blister called.

"May we really?"

"Shame not to, I think." Blister took an enameled case from one pocket, flicked it open, and selected a pine match that flared with a green tinge and a whiff of sulfur when he struck it against the box.

"Ooh," Liao said. "*Fā zhú!* Can I try one?"

"Be my guest." Blister handed the box to Liao and took the incendiary. "*Fā zhú*, you said?"

"Liao makes matches that light from friction too," Lucy said. "We sometimes use them in place of quick-match aboard the *Fate*. He makes our slow-match, too. Better than anything anyone else has, Papa says."

"But my *fā zhú* aren't as nice as these," Liao said, striking one. He watched the greenish flame, transfixed, for so long that it burned down to his fingers before he appeared to remember that he'd lit it in order to light the little explosive's fuse. "Oh, I'm sorry," he said, looking up at Blister. "I wasted one."

"No matter," Blister said airily. "I have plenty. You may have a box yourself, if you like." He bowed to Lucy. "If it's all right, that is."

Lucy shrugged. "I can't see the point of refusing him matches when he can make his own."

Liao took another from the box and struck it to life. Blister handed him the blue sphere and Liao whipped the tip of the match across the fuse with the neat and confident speed of someone who was well accustomed to lighting combustibles. Then he drew back his arm and flung the ball into the air. Blister caught Trigemine's eye as the incendiary headed for its apex, and over his open, friendly smile, his eyes hardened just a bit. *Look, now,* the expression said. *Now we shall see what we shall see.*

The thing stopped rising and the little spark trailing along its fuse disappeared. Then the ball exploded and a curled red tangle erupted from within. It unwound itself immediately, explosively, bringing to mind a gadget Trigemine had seen on one of his journeys: a spring covered in thin fabric painted to resemble a snake that burst from a tin can when the lid was removed. Except the tail of this snake was on fire, and the blaze rushed along its length: bright red flames that hissed loudly enough to be audible below. The coruscating serpent writhed thirty feet overhead for a second like a tiny wingless dragon, and then with a pop it dissolved into a fizz of golden sparks and tiny shreds of red and blue paper that rained down like smoke-scented confetti. All this took thirty seconds from beginning to end.

Trigemine whistled, and it took no acting on his part to sound impressed. "You made that?" Liao beamed, holding up one small palm to catch bits of the tattered paper as if they were snowflakes. "But you were in there for only fifteen minutes or so. Weren't they?" he asked Lucy. She nodded, looking a bit smug and not in the least surprised.

"Twelve," Blister corrected. "I had my eye on the clock the entire time."

"You've made those . . . those objects before, then."

Liao shook his head, spilling paper bits from hand to hand. "I've never had this sort of . . ." He turned to Blister. "It's *qiān huánghuá* at home. What is it in the English?"

"Red massicot."

"Well, red massicot is uncommon, so I've never actually used it, but Mr. Blister has some and I thought perhaps —" There followed what Trigemine assumed was a highly technical account of how Liao had arrived at the means for crafting the serpent, delivered in an incomprehensible mix of chemical English and Latin, plus Chinese when the boy didn't have English or Latin terms for what he wanted to say. Blister, however, was evidently following the explanation perfectly, because he kept shooting significant glances at Trigemine over the boy's head.

They had found their conflagrationeer.

Blister and Liao turned to the rest of the incendiaries they'd brought from the wagon and spent the next fifteen minutes detonating them. Trigemine kept an eye on the road back to the Harbors, certain that the noise would bring curious spectators. But in the midday sun the explosions of light were only just visible, and mercifully nothing set fire to the trees, so the four of them were still alone when the last little rocket sent blue sparks raining down among them.

"What a thumping great blue," Liao breathed. "How did you make it?"

Blister made a production of consulting his watch. "I should love to tell you, Liao, but sadly Mr. Trigemine and I are out of time. Perhaps it would be better at any rate to show you."

He turned to Lucy. "What say you to this idea, Miss Bluecrowne? You mentioned that Liao has his very own workshop at your house. Supposing tomorrow I bring what's needed for the blue up to the workshop, along with a few other things your brother might find amusing? I could teach Liao how to compound them himself."

"Not tomorrow," Trigemine said quickly. If Blister was right and they were going to have to kidnap the boy, he needed time to resolve the issue of the Albatross first.

"Of course, not tomorrow. The day after, perhaps?" Blister glanced at him.

Trigemine considered. Two days ought to do it. "Certainly."

"We live on the hill. You would come all the way up just to teach Liao a blue?" Lucy asked, surprised.

Blister put a finger to his nose. "Well, I am a man of business, so I shan't do it for free. It will cost you a dinner basket, and I shall insist upon having some sort of homemade cakes. I am excessively fond of homemade cakes."

A flicker of panic crossed Lucy's face. Trigemine nearly laughed. "Certainly ladies brought up on privateers—excuse me, letters-of-marque—have better things to do than learn to bake," he said. "Have pity."

"My terms are not negotiable," Blister said airily. "But as long as they're baked in someone's home, I shall consider the condition met. What sort of thing do you like best to drink at dinner?" he asked Liao.

"Seven-water grog," Liao said immediately.

"Which is what?"

Lucy spoke up. "Grog is rum and water. Seven-water grog is . . . well, it has quite a bit more water than the usual proportions."

"Then I should like the basket to include a jug of seven-water grog." Blister winked at Liao. "Compounding is thirsty work."

"A dinner basket with homemade-somewhere cakes and seven-water grog it is, then," the girl said. She and Blister shook hands. "Shall I draw you a map?"

"If you please. I'll just get a bit of paper." When Blister returned from the wagon, he had paper, a pencil, and a small lamp on a chain. He handed the writing implements to Lucy and held up the lamp. "Liao mentioned that you have just acquired a boat. Perhaps you will find this useful. A gift."

Trigemine kept an eye on Lucy's face as Blister explained the provenance of the lamp in an elaborate and fanciful story that sounded quite a lot like a fairy tale. She listened politely as she drew a map to the house on the hill, but she showed no reaction to the tale itself. "A gift for me?" she asked when Blister finished. "Why?"

Smart girl, Trigemine thought.

Blister gave her his most congenial smile. "Because I haven't had such a stimulating afternoon in a very long time. And because I am looking forward to cake."

They fixed the meeting for one o'clock in the afternoon in two days' time. Then the two children took their leave, Liao bouncing along and turning back to wave every few steps, and Lucy with the lamp under one elbow, striding riverward as if drawn to the water by some great magnet. "A gift for the girl?" Trigemine asked as they watched the small figures disappear.

"Very important, that. I need to know more about the boy. I'm certain that there's something different about him." Blister's countenance took on a wary cast. "The things he knows, Foulk. Extraordinary."

"But isn't that to be expected? After all, we did come in search of a conflagrationeer."

"It's more. There's *something* more. I need to know what that something is."

"And the lamp will tell you . . . how?"

"I'll show you. But later."

"All right." Trigemine tucked his hands in his pockets. Now all that remained was the Albatross.

"The boat was a good idea, wasn't it?" Liao said breathlessly as he and Lucy trooped up the final steps to the gate at the top of the hill.

"A capital idea," Lucy huffed. She turned to peer over the railing at the little cutter moored at the pier below. "She's perfect, Liao. Isn't she perfect?"

Of course, really she was far from that. She would need plenty of work, and Lucy couldn't wait to begin. She patted the pocket of her skirt, where the action list she and the bosun had made crinkled cheerfully. Tomorrow: cleaning out the hull and sanding down everything inside. Day after: recaulking all the old seams. And soon—but not soon enough—fresh paint for the whole. She would make do with whatever the *Fate* could rustle up spare—which meant green—but maroon would certainly look handsome.

"Will you put Mr. Blister's lantern on the *Driven Star*?"

"Can't have an open flame on a boat. But perhaps we could hang it here at the top of the climb. Make it our home light." She took her ditty bag from her shoulder, pulled the little lamp from within, and hung it from a lantern hook on the side of the gate. "There!"

"It wants oil."

"We can bring some out later and see how it burns."

"I had another idea, you know," Liao said in a contemplative tone.

She tried not to laugh at the serious expression on his little face, which was still red from the climb. When he looked at her like that, it was easy to forget he was only seven. "What is it, Liao?"

"It's about the house," Liao said. "Papa said perhaps if I asked you nicely, you might tell me about it."

Lucy snorted. "How? It's as new to me as it is to you. I don't know anything about this place." *And I don't want to know,* she added silently.

His face fell. "But Papa said you would have stories about it."

"How could I have stories? I saw it for the first time only a few minutes before you did."

"Yes, I remember." He frowned, confused, as they crossed the lawn. "Now I don't understand."

Lucy frowned too, trying to figure out what Captain Bluecrowne could possibly have meant. Something to do with the heirloom windows, perhaps?

By the time they'd gone inside, she still hadn't figured it out. While Liao ran to the kitchen in search of a snack of ship's biscuit, she climbed up into the seat in one of the bow windows and leaned her elbows on her knees. What on earth was her father thinking of?

That strange sense of familiarity she'd noticed when they'd first arrived came creeping back. She gazed out the window and found herself picturing a cobbled street with a harbor beyond it in place of the lawn and trees. *Malta,* Lucy realized with a jolt. There *was* something familiar about this window seat, even with the unfamiliar view on the other side of the glass. More than once she'd sat in a very similar bow window when the *Left-Handed Fate* had put into the island of Malta and her father had rented rooms in a house on a street that fronted the harbor.

"I believe I know what he meant," Lucy said slowly, touching the glass as Liao returned. "This window was built to be very like the ones in a house in Malta where Papa and I stayed now and then."

Liao climbed up and sat in the other corner. "What is Malta?"

"It's an island in the Mediterranean. Bonaparte conquered it for a while, but then his soldiers were driven out and now it's a British dominion. His Majesty's ships often stop there."

"And the *Fate*?"

"The *Fate*, as well. Usually captains sleep aboard ship when in port, but sometimes for a change of scenery Papa and I would stay ashore in Malta, at Mrs. Allyn's house. I used to like to sit in a window just like this and take in the goings-on down on the water." She waved across the lawn near the house. "That would've been a road made of big, flat rectangular stones. And there would be horses and carts and groups of sailors walking along it, and ladies in faldettas that catch the breezes like great black sails."

Liao was leaning on his own knees now. "Ladies wear *black sails* in this place?"

"No, faldettas are great dark cloaks with huge hoods. But in a breeze they billow a bit like a sail does."

"So this house is like Malta," Liao said, looking around.

Lucy followed his eyes. "No, not the whole house." Where had she been when she'd felt that earlier twinge of familiarity? "Come with me."

They went outside, Liao trooping along in Lucy's shadow as she crossed the lawn. She turned back, and the twinge came again. She examined the façade inch by inch, searching for the source of the feeling, and this time she found it: the clock-tower shape of the upper floors. "Well, I'll be—the tall middle bit, do you see? That's just like a house I remember in Riga. Riga is a city on a gulf in the Baltic Sea. Papa sometimes goes there for canvas and cordage."

"Cordage is ropes," Liao said confidently.

"Exactly right. In Riga they make the very *best* cordage. And in Riga, there's a house—three of them, all in a line, that look very much like that." A lump rose in her throat as she remembered how she'd fallen in love with the three houses in their neat row: one green, one yellow, and one white.

There were more memories to be found, now that Lucy knew to seek them out: memories hidden in the design of the porch, the shapes of the dormers, even the particular color of the front door. And it wasn't only Lucy's memories that had been built into the house. Liao began finding things too. He had just declared delightedly that the tiled roof was exactly like the one atop a temple back home when Lucy remembered the suggestion Xiaoming had made that morning. *Consider what it would take to make this place at least somewhat homelike, even if you think it can never truly be home.*

"We should give the house a name," Lucy said, looking up at it.

"A name for the house? It's called *house* already!" Liao started to laugh, then stopped and nodded soberly. "Oh, yes, I see. Like the carpenter is called Chips because he is the carpenter, but his proper name is Mr. Raines. Or like Papa's ship. She's called a schooner because that's what sort of thing she is, but her proper name is the *Left-Handed Fate*."

"Yes, exactly."

"Lucy and Liao's Riga House," Liao suggested promptly.

Lucy raised her eyebrows. "Well . . . that's quite good, but perhaps it should be something that lets Jìmǔ know it is her house as well."

"And Papa's, too," Liao added. "All of ours, even when we aren't all here. Because we are a *family,* and it is our *family* house."

He'd spoken as if working through mathematics, but there had been a hopeful quality to his words too. As if he was afraid she would correct him on some part of it and was hoping she would not. Hoping that he was right and that they *were* a family, despite their differences. Hoping that even if Lucy got her wish and went back to sea with their father, that they would come back, and when they did, the four of them would be a family once more. Every time.

A sudden rush of affection for her brother crested over Lucy. "That's right," she said softly, and she put a hand on his shoulder, because it seemed that some sort of comforting touch was in order. "That's just exactly right, Liao."

"Then should we not call it Bluecrowne? Because that is our family name?"

"Well . . ." This was more difficult. On the one hand, Lucy was pleased that Liao felt that taking Richard Bluecrowne's surname meant an extra connection rather than the loss of anything—that it was, perhaps, like adding a pennant rather than striking one's colors to run up someone else's flag. On the other hand, *Bluecrowne* didn't quite do the job the way she'd imagined. But it would be a shame to disappoint Liao, who seemed to think it was perfect because it was the name they all now shared.

"I say, Liao," she said slowly, "could you . . . could you render Bluecrowne into the Chinese? Translate the words *blue* and *crown*? Perhaps we could call the house that."

"Why?"

"Because then, you see, it would be even more special, wouldn't it? Because it would mix up both the English and the Chinese parts of our family, all into one."

"Oh!" Liao brightened. "I see." He thought for a moment. "I can, yes."

"Well, write down the symbols, will you? Perhaps the carpenter can put together something in the way of a sign, and we can surprise Papa and Jìmǔ."

"This is a good idea," Liao said seriously. "When it has a name—*our* name—then it will be our house for true."

Perhaps, Lucy thought, she wasn't the only one struggling with the idea of staying behind. "Then it will be our house for true," she repeated, hoping it sounded as if she meant it.

EIGHT

THE HALO

HAT is your plan, then?" Trigemine asked as he and Blister hiked up the road to the Quenching Press late that afternoon.

They had just concluded their meeting with the gunner of the *Left-Handed Fate,* who was so proud of the little prodigy Liao that he had required only the slightest prompting to talk about him. He had confirmed that the boy had learned some of his craft from the family of his Chinese mother and that the lady herself had come to Nagspeake with the *Left-Handed Fate.* Goodness, no, she didn't trifle with incendiaries, not according to Mr. Harrick. She was a proper lady, was Lady Xiaoming. Foreign, of course, but proper.

"My plan?" Blister shrugged. "Blow up the workshop and walk out with the boy. Something of that nature."

"You make it sound so very simple."

"I see no reason why it shouldn't be. I shall have to know more about his mother, just in case, but the lamp will take care of that." Blister seemed uneasy for a moment, then shook his head. "The lamp will tell. No point in worrying until then."

"Go back to the bit about blowing up the workshop. How will you keep from blowing up yourself and the boy in the process?" That earned Trigemine a disappointed, even insulted look from his companion as they stepped into the tavern. Trigemine only half noticed. His attention was diverted almost immediately to the bar, where the tall figure of Christopher Swifte sat in conversation with another man.

"I am a complete salamander, Foulk," Blister said reproachfully, lowering his voice. "Fire is my natural element. As for the boy— that's merely a matter of an easy anti-inflammatory elixir. I imagine I probably sold some to Jack Hellcoal himself along with the vitriol, if you saw him walk through fire. Why do you think I asked for the boy's favorite drink? I need only make certain it won't be tasted in watered-down rum. That's simple enough."

Trigemine glanced sharply back at Blister. *"Simple enough?"* So blowing up a building with himself in it without taking damage and turning a small boy fireproof so he could walk through fire as well fell into the category of things that were *simple enough*. That was faintly disturbing.

"Mr. Trigemine." The peddlers turned toward the bar, where the Ironmonger caught Trigemine's eye and jerked his head at the stool to his left.

"I'll be upstairs," Blister said. "See if the barkeep will send up something approximating seven-water grog so I know what I'm working with." Then he tipped his hat to Swifte and headed for one of the gilded lifts.

Trigemine bowed shortly, swept his hat from his head, and slid onto the stool beside the Ironmonger. The fellow Swifte had been speaking to was still there, but he'd moved a little way down the bar and was apparently immersed in a broadsheet. Apart from him, they were alone. "Mr. Swifte. May I buy you another tumbler of whatever you're having there?"

"If you like, but I've decided not to sell to you," Swifte said without preamble. Trigemine stiffened in the act of signaling the man behind the bar. "I don't know but you might regret buying me a drink if I don't tell you so right up front."

The bartender appeared with annoying promptness. "You'll have what, sir?"

"Whisky and quinine," Trigemine said, recovering himself. "And refill the gentleman's glass."

The barman blinked, confused. "Quinine?"

Trigemine sighed. Too early in the century. "Just the whisky." As the barkeep turned to the row of bottles behind him, Trigemine faced the Ironmonger. "Mind if I ask why?"

"Came down to the question of whether I wanted to make any more blades like this one."

"And you don't."

"And I don't." He rubbed the scar below his left ear as the barman poured Trigemine two inches of liquor, then refilled Swifte's tumbler from an older, dustier bottle. "It takes more than I want to give to do it again."

"More than you want to give Morvengarde?"

"More than I want to give anyone." He picked up his glass, his broad, scarred hand dwarfing it, as if it were a child's cup.

Trigemine's eyes flicked to the lapel beneath which Swifte was presumably still carrying the Albatross in its leather sheath. "Sell me the one, then."

"No." Swifte set his glass down gently, but his voice was hard as marble.

"And may I ask why not?"

"You ask a lot of questions of strangers, don't you?"

"If I'm going to have to tell Morvengarde I wasn't able to bring back what he sent me for, I'm damn well going to know the reason. Not that it'll make any odds what that reason is," Trigemine added darkly. "Won't matter to Morvengarde, anyhow, but he'll still ask."

Swifte grinned. "No, I don't imagine it will. Fine, then. You need an explanation to give to the man in charge, you tell him I refused to sell my knife because I'm not going to make any more and sometimes a man likes to keep the things he's made."

"You're not going to make . . . what? Any more Albatrosses, or any more knives at all?"

The Ironmonger's grin thinned. He drank again, deeper this time. "Any more weapons."

"*Ever?*"

"Ever."

Trigemine cursed silently and furiously. This, *this* was why the journey had been so carefully timed. The confluence of the Ironmonger and the mystery conflagrationeer was part of it, but it was also simply a matter of the Ironmonger's particular chronology: by Trigemine's own era in the latter half of the century, the legendary weapons-maker had, in fact, done exactly this. He had left both his profession and the roaming world, and he had put down roots.

But it wasn't supposed to happen *yet*.

This had to be about the Jumper. The Jumper had not figured into Trigemine's always exhaustive reckonings, and somehow his presence had changed the Ironmonger's life.

"Will you be selling it to the other buyer, then?" Trigemine asked when he was certain his anger wouldn't ring in his words.

"I said I was keeping it." Swifte emptied his tumbler. "And I'm keeping it." He got to his feet and glanced down at Trigemine from his full height. "But I thank you for the drink. Safe travels."

And with that, Christopher Swifte strode from the Quenching Press and disappeared into the deep golden glare of the sinking sun. Trigemine stifled a howl of fury. He downed his drink, waved the barman over again, and asked for a jug of seven-water grog to be sent up to Blister's quarters. "Yes, I really want a jug of very weak rum," he snarled. "And I'll have another of these." The barkeep shrugged and picked up the whisky bottle. "Not that one. I'll have what Swifte was drinking." Trigemine glanced over at the other man at the bar, who wore a frankly amused expression on his face. "Can I help you?"

The stranger let out a low, *Have a look at this fellow* whistle and turned away with a chuckle to go back to the broadsheet he had been reading.

Trigemine sighed and took a sip from his refilled glass, then stared down into it, momentarily distracted. Whatever was in that old bottle, it was amazing.

As the liquor simmered its way down his throat, he considered the man with the broadsheet out of the corner of his eye. Trigemine remembered seeing him in the Quenching Press the day before. Like the boy conflagrationeer, he looked to be from points east and wore a long, braided pigtail; maybe he, too, was Chinese. On the other hand, most of the sailors in the Harbors had pigtails, so perhaps that wasn't—

"Can I help you?" the man said without raising his eyes.

"Guess I wasn't being as subtle as I thought." Trigemine waved at the barman again and tapped his glass. "One of these for my friend here."

The barkeep lifted an eyebrow and wordlessly poured the stranger a slug. Counting the drink he'd stood Swifte, that made three hits from the old bottle, and something about the glance that passed between the barkeep and the other guy told Trigemine that he was running up a bigger bill than he'd planned.

"Generous," the pigtailed man said. "I hear there's not much of this stuff left around."

Trigemine silently reminded himself that he had an allowance for expenses, and made his face friendly. "Foulk Trigemine," he said, holding out his hand.

"Jianming Cerrajero." They shook.

"So, where you from, Mr. Cerrajero?" This was confusing. Was the man Chinese or of Latin American descent?

"I'm from here," the stranger said darkly. "Where are *you* from?"

"Apologies," Trigemine said. "I'm from the States."

"Ah." The stranger took a drink. "A foreigner, then."

"You might say so." Trigemine gave up trying to regain his poise. "I'm in town looking for someone originally from . . ." What had Blister said earlier? "Canton. Pretty new in town. And I'll admit I wondered if you might know them, seeing as the Harbors aren't all that big a place."

"Figure all the Chinese folks in town probably get to know each other pretty fast, do you?" Cerrajero took another drink. "I doubt I know the fellow, but what's his name?"

"Hers. It's Xiaoming. Lady Xiaoming Bluecrowne, I believe."

Cerrajero hesitated over his drink, and something about the fleeting expression that crossed his face made Trigemine pay closer attention.

"Xiaoming's a boy's name," Cerrajero said, finally. "You must be mistaken."

"I'm not."

Again, Cerrajero hesitated in that very interesting way. "Well, I can't help you. The only female Xiaoming I've ever heard of comes from a . . . I think you'd say a folktale."

"So if I'm trying to find a youngish woman married to a British sea captain, she wouldn't be the girl I'm after."

"She'd be a few thousand years old," Cerrajero said. "And

somehow I don't see a mythical Chinese princess turning up in Nagspeake. Though we do get all kinds here." There was a dismissive note in the other man's tone that made Trigemine suspect that that last comment was probably directed at him. Cerrajero polished off what was left in his glass, collected his paper, and stood up. "Thanks for the drink." He saluted the barman and ambled out the door.

Trigemine asked for his bill, cursed when he got it, and drained his own glass, barking "Send the grog up" as he stalked across the tavern to the nearest lift.

A faintly acrid smell wafted out from beneath Blister's door. It reminded Trigemine a bit of the odor that hung smoky and low over a battlefield, yet at the same time it brought to mind something floral and cloying. Crushed roses, or something in that line.

He rapped on the door with his knuckles, and a moment later, Blister opened it just a crack. "Grog's on its way," Trigemine said. "What is that smell?"

"You look as though you've been kicked." Blister stepped aside. "But you're just in time. The lamp is about to report."

Trigemine followed him into the darkened room, illuminated only by what little of the oncoming sunset managed to fight through the closed shutters. "The lamp you gave the Bluecrowne girl?"

"Indeed."

A different lamp stood on a table in the middle of the space. It was unlit, but even in the gloom Trigemine could see the air around it shimmering faintly, the way air shimmers around a flame. "How does this work?" he asked. "That lamp's different from the girl's."

"It's not the lamp that matters. I could've used any lamp at all. It's merely a vessel for a special wick that burns with a very particular blaze." He pulled a chair up to the table and sat. "Tanglefire," he said reverently.

"Tanglefire?"

The peddler nodded. "The wick in this lamp and the wick in the girl's were made together under very particular conditions, and the flames they produce when lit are connected."

"You mean if you light this one, that one lights too? Won't that cause some comment, a lamp suddenly coming to life?"

"It would, if it were that simple. If she lights the lamp, she'll see a blue flame. Not ordinary fire, no, but at least fire that comes and goes as she'd expect." Blister passed a hand over the top of the wick and winced. "But the light of tanglefire is invisible to the naked eye. If I light the girl's lamp by lighting mine, there will be nothing for her to see." Blister reached into his coat, withdrew a pair of spectacles with amber lenses, and passed them to Trigemine. "Put these on." Then he raised his scissors-glasses to his own eyes and turned toward the invisible flame.

Trigemine dragged another chair over to the table, unfolded the specs, and set them on his nose. Immediately, the room changed. Or rather, the room remained, but now it contained another place within it. This new place wavered in the light of an unmoving single flame the color of straw that burned at the end of the wick. He was reminded of the way people and things could emerge suddenly from a thick mist, and how light caught in a mist like that could seem a bit like an insect caught in amber.

The new place was outdoors: a wooden platform surrounded by a stand of birches and those peculiar firs that Trigemine had only ever seen in Nagspeake. Then he realized he couldn't actually see the gold of the leaves or the blue-green of the pine needles. The world revealed by the tanglefire had a bleached quality to it, as if everything visible had been carved from driftwood and charcoal.

Lucy and Liao Bluecrowne sat on the platform. They were talking, but Trigemine couldn't hear their words. They raised their heads, their gazes skipping over the watching peddlers without seeing them, and Liao raised a hand to wave. Trigemine turned and saw a very beautiful young woman coming across a lawn that stretched from the trees to a bizarre house with a scattering of stained-glass windows. The captain's wife, presumably. Lady Xiaoming.

Beside him, Blister made a noise. Behind the lenses of his scissors-glasses, his eyes were worried, and glued to the young woman.

Liao ran to his mother and hugged her tightly. Beyond the unusualness of finding a woman who looked like that in a place like this, there was nothing about Lady Xiaoming that suggested anything uncommon to Trigemine. They did get all kinds in Nagspeake, as the man at the bar had said.

And yet . . . thinking of that odd hesitation on Cerrajero's face, Trigemine reached into his pocket. Beside the kairos mechanism he found the round shape of a jeweler's loupe. He pulled the spectacles away just far enough to pop the loupe into the cavity of one eye.

Aha.

Now the boy's mother stood out from the bleached world as if she had been outlined in silver. It could mean any of several things, but it undoubtedly signified that this woman was different. Special. The kind of special Morvengarde could get exceptionally good money for.

There was a tap on his shoulder, and beside him Blister lowered the scissors-glasses. Trigemine lowered his own specs and removed the loupe, and the bleached world disappeared, leaving the two peddlers alone in a dim room.

"The woman," Blister said, his face a mask of disbelief. "What did you see?"

"A halo," Trigemine answered, wishing he'd gotten more out of Cerrajero before the man had left. *The only female Xiaoming I've ever heard of comes from a . . . I think you'd say a folktale.* "She's what Morvengarde would call a reliquary."

"Meaning what?"

Trigemine smiled grimly. "Meaning she could be taken apart into a number of very useful and profitable relics. What'd *you* see?"

"Something I've never seen before. But I know what she is." Blister sat back. "Unbelievable." He put his palm to his mouth. After a moment he looked at Trigemine again. "The much-admired proper lady, Lady Xiaoming, is, shall we say, not what she appears."

"Not a proper lady after all?"

"Not *human,*" Blister said grimly. "Or at least, not merely. Couldn't you tell? The halo, after all."

"A halo can mean many things. In my experience, mainly it means she's valuable." Trigemine tapped his fingers on the table, thinking hard. "There was a man downstairs," he said at length, and proceeded to recount his brief conversation with Cerrajero. "Whoever—*whatever* she is, if we could take her, too, Morvengarde would be over the moon." Over the moon, yes, but at the same time he would still be furious if Trigemine didn't come back with the Albatross. Trigemine pushed that thought out of his head. One problem at a time. "Tell me more about the not-merely-human bit."

"Well, what I know of Chinese roamers is limited, so I can't say precisely what sort of being she is, but certainly she's no mere mortal. She's something more like one of us—a presence that doesn't walk the usual paths of time, and with more than the usual capabilities at her disposal. But she's on an entirely different level than you or I. *Yǔrén*, perhaps . . . or maybe *rénxiān* . . . or some other sort of entity entirely. I couldn't say."

"You mean she's strong? Powerful? What's a *yǔrén*?"

"It's not precisely the right term, but you could use the word *immortal* if you wanted and you wouldn't be far wrong," Blister said. "And yes, she will be incredibly, *vastly* powerful, if we're forced to face her."

"Immortal," Trigemine repeated. "Roaming-world immortal or actual immortal? Long life, or honest-to-God won't die?"

"I don't know. Either? Both? Anyhow, thank goodness you bought us an extra day. This . . . this changes things." Blister rubbed his face. "I need to study how one handles this sort of being, if one finds oneself in opposition to them. She will come after her son, and it will not be pretty. But on the other hand, I'd wager any sum that the boy inherited his skill with fire from his mother. As a conflagrationeer, she could probably conjure a fire for Jack Hellcoal the likes of which even the Devil has never seen."

"But what are *our* chances against her, then?"

"I honestly don't know," Blister said simply. "But if we can't best her, we're sunk. We'll never escape with her son as long as she's in play." He glanced at Trigemine. "I suppose you have some math to do."

"You might say so." Trigemine sighed and patted his vest pocket. "You're going to have to give me some information first, but I seem to be missing my notebook. I imagine it's in my room." He went to the door, and when he opened it, a young man carrying a jug cringed away. "Hello there," Trigemine said, eyes narrowing.

The fellow flinched. He was seventeen or so, barely more than a boy. Who knew how much he'd heard? He certainly couldn't have understood it all, but he'd gotten enough of the gist of it to be nervous. Trigemine glanced past him into the hallway. There was no one else in view. He indicated the jug with a jerk of his chin. "I believe that's for us?"

"Seven-water grog," the boy said, stammering a bit on the *seven*. Yep. He'd heard enough.

"Just set it there, will you?" Trigemine said, pointing to the little table by the door. Inside, but not so far inside that the kid would balk and refuse to come in. Meanwhile, he ran rapid numbers in his head. The mathematics were a bit knotty to do off the cuff, and there were absolutely going to be repercussions he couldn't anticipate, but the fact that he was about to have to recalculate the entire mission made it easier to throw caution toward the wind.

The boy swallowed and stepped over the threshold to set the jug on the table. Trigemine reached into his watch pocket. He took two pins from the pincushion, then thumbed open the kairos mechanism and felt it unfold. One quick motion to place a pin into the mechanism and another to jab the remaining one through the young man's collar, and the thing was done.

He yelped; Trigemine must've caught the skin of his neck. But it didn't matter. They were no longer in either Nagspeake or 1810.

The boy's body carried him instinctively toward the place where the door had been, but now there was only the swirling mist of daybreak, and it was scented with spring instead of autumn. Shouts and footfalls sounded from behind, and the boy whirled to see flashes of red-coated figures running toward him.

"Don't be afraid," Trigemine said soothingly. "They will say later that it happened at Concord, the one that was heard round the world, but the truth is that the shot that kills you here will be the first." He pointed, and the boy's wild eyes followed his finger. "From that tavern, right there."

The boy's eyes went wide and frantic, but before he could speak or move, there was the distinct *pop* of a musket shot. And then he jolted, flinging his arms forward in an oddly graceful, swanlike flap as first his head and then his body flew backward.

Trigemine had returned to the room at the Quenching Press before the boy's body hit the ground. "Everything all right?" Blister asked from the table.

"Just fine." Trigemine folded the kairos mechanism closed and buttoned his jacket over it. "I'll just go find my notes, and then we can get to work."

Returning from his own room, he met the barkeep walking toward Blister's. "Seen my boy?" he asked.

Trigemine tilted his head. "Your boy?"

"I sent him up with grog, as you asked. He hasn't come back."

"Well, he did bring the grog—that much I can tell you." Trigemine rapped on Blister's door, waited for the peddler's answering "Come in," and opened it. "But I haven't seen him since he left." He made a production of standing aside so the barman could see for himself that there was no one but Blister in the room.

The man eyed the jug on the table. "Odd. Well, he'll turn up. Night, gents."

"Good night," Trigemine replied, and closed the door.

NINE

CHRONOMETRICAL TRIGONOMETRY

LUCY woke to bells. The tolling came from below, and even though there was only the ground floor beneath this one, the peals sounded so far away that she wasn't even certain how many times the bell had been rung. She crawled out of her hammock, which she had slung over the uncomfortably stable bed the night before, and stared in disbelief at the mahogany timepiece on her desk. Eight a.m.: time for breakfast.

She dressed quickly in a worn blue shirt and a pair of nankeen trousers, then tucked her task list in one pocket—though she had read it over so many times that it was mostly memorized. Then she hurried down to the galley. *The kitchen,* she corrected herself as she took the stairs two at a time.

Lucy tried to be civil and attentive during breakfast and to eat like a reasonably well-bred human, but she doubted she was making much of a job of it. Her father and Xiaoming exchanged amused and knowing looks. Liao watched her with frank amazement. She didn't care. There was a boat down at the house's little dock, and that boat was waiting for her.

She gulped the last of her coffee and excused herself, and then she was flying across the lawn, pulling on her canvas jacket as she went. She descended the seemingly endless flight of stairs, and there was the cutter, at once completely ragged and utterly beautiful as she bobbed under the trees that sheltered the pier.

A mass of supplies had been brought from the *Fate*, heaped on the pier, and covered with tarpaulin. Lucy perched on an outcropping of the pile and considered her prize. *My very own boat.*

A part of her tried to rebel against the rush of pleasure that came with the thought. *Stay angry,* that part insisted. *Don't let yourself be bought so easily!*

I am *still angry,* Lucy told herself. *But I am also here, and so is this sweet little barky.* She got to her feet, tugged the *Driven Star* by its mooring line until its side bumped gently against the pier, and stepped gingerly down into it.

She hauled on the halyard and inspected the sail as it climbed, noting all the places where the sun peeked through a collection of minute tears and holes in the canvas. But the old sail caught the breeze nonetheless, and the *Driven Star* rocked gently, as if eager to be cast loose from her moorings and taken out for a jaunt. That suited Lucy; there might be a new sail coming, but she wasn't planning on waiting for it before her next cruise.

"Soon," Lucy said, patting the gunwale. "Soon, I promise."

Despite having been kept under the wharf, the boat was full of debris: dirt, moss, tattered spider's webs, old paper scraps, and several seasons' worth of leaves and dead bugs. The first thing on the list was a thorough cleaning-out of the hull. Lucy leapt back onto the pier, found a spade and a short-handled broom in the supply pile, and got to work. "We'll rant and we'll roar like true British sailors," she sang as she swept. "We'll rant and we'll roar all on the salt seas!"

Cleaning out the cutter took longer than she'd anticipated, and it felt as though she had only just begun sanding down the inside surfaces with a small holystone when she heard quick feet tromping across the pier. "Lucy!" Liao shouted. "It's noon! Garvett sent a dinner basket!"

How had four hours passed so quickly? she wondered as she wiped wood dust from her face and climbed out of the cutter to help Liao with the basket he had carried down on his back.

He plopped to a cross-legged seat beside it, fished a square of hardtack from within, and rapped the biscuit smartly against the pier several times. "How is it coming along?" he inquired of Lucy as he leaned down to survey the leisurely escape of the weevils he'd knocked loose. "What comes after the blessed rock?"

"*Holystone,* Liao, not blessed rock." She found a sandwich of cold ham and soft-tack in the basket and took a ravenous bite. Holystoning was hungry work. "The next thing's to caulk the seams with new oakum, only I shan't get to that today." She paused, chewing. "It's slow going."

But this wasn't really a complaint. Lucy had spent an entire watch aboard the *Driven Star* now, and as she'd swept and emptied and holystoned she'd been getting to know the little vessel: how she bore weight, where the seams creaked, how she rode in the water—all manner of small but significant clues to her personality.

Liao poured cold cider from a jug into a cup and sank the half-chewed hardtack square into it. "When can we take her out again?"

"Anytime we like, I suppose." Lucy scratched sand and dust from her hair. "There's no water coming in that I can find. And though she badly needs a new sail, this one did get us here from the Harbors, so I suppose it'll do for short trips." She looked up from her ham biscuit. "Why?"

The boy's gaze had shifted from the weevils on the worn wooden planks to the pile of supplies under the tarpaulin. "I think I see some barrels of my powder under there."

"It's midday," Lucy pointed out. "Surely there would be nothing to see."

Liao gave her a reproachful look. "I could make *something* we could see."

Beside them, the *Driven Star* rocked, thudding softly against the pier and sending ripples into the reflections on the river. *Come,* she whispered, beckoning with a flutter of her patchwork sail. *Come, let us have a short cruise to shake the dust from my timbers. You have all the time in the world for prettying, but this day will only last until nightfall.*

Lucy's face broke into a broad grin. "All right. Get what you need and we'll take her for a jaunt."

Liao downed his cider and leapt to his feet. He peeked at the barrels under the canvas, returned to the basket for a ham biscuit, then ran for the stairs. "Back quick and quick, Lucy!"

She chuckled and finished her own dinner, then returned to holystoning. She had just gotten into a sort of mindless rhythm when a small barrel rolled straight off the pier and dropped into the bottom of the cutter. "What on earth?"

"It's time for our jaunt!" Liao called, busily untying the mooring line at the bow. He half climbed, half fell into the boat, then ordered, "Take us out!" as he got to his feet and checked the bag slung across his chest to be certain nothing had fallen out. "I have everything I need here. I'll do the rest as you sail."

Lucy laughed and leaned over the side to rinse the dust from her arms, then made her way aft to the tiller. "All right, then. Cast off the other line."

The *Driven Star* slid eagerly out onto the Skidwrack. Lucy had gotten to know her sailing qualities a bit the day before, both on the way to the *Fate* and on the way back to the house, but Kendrick had been there both times. This, then, was her first trip as the most senior sailor aboard. It was daunting for half a minute, and then there was only the river, the breeze, the cutter, and Lucy. The tiller and the shabby sail translated those four marine dialects into a smooth-flowing poem of motion. And, of course, there was Liao, fidgeting in the bow, sifting and measuring, twisting paper and murmuring to himself in languages Lucy didn't know.

She took the *Driven Star* upriver beyond the cliff to where the ground began to slope more gently. Here the pines leaned out over the Skidwrack at seemingly impossible angles, dipping boughs into the water like delicate fingers. "How's this?" Lucy called to her brother.

Liao licked a finger, touched it to his nose, and tilted his head back, gauging the wind. "This will do." Then he opened a telescoping stand that he'd often used on the *Fate,* fitted a small rocket into it, and lit the fuse with one of Blister's matches. "Here's to our new boat, Lucy!" he shouted as the red glow climbed the fuse.

The rocket sailed skyward. When it exploded, a shower of deep magenta drifted down over the *Driven Star,* opaque enough to be perfectly visible in the afternoon sky. There was little sparkle or glow to this starburst—or at least, the sky was too bright for much sparkle to show. Instead, the shower was like a rain of wet, darkly gleaming flower petals that shone as they descended as if they had been caught in a beam of sunlight.

"Oh, Liao!" Lucy reached out a hand instinctively, trying to catch one of the petals before it slipped out of existence, but of course nothing survived to fall into her palm. "I've never seen the like! Where did you learn that?"

"I've been thinking about how to do it." Liao fitted another rocket into the stand and lit the fuse. "It's mostly a matter of contrast. The color must be dark and dense." The second rocket burst with a sound like a drum the size of a lake, and the starburst overhead made Lucy think of a pumpkin-colored chrysanthemum flying to pieces in all directions.

She clapped her hands. "How magnificent! Why have you never shown me these before?"

Liao's face clouded over as he studied his handiwork. "Because it isn't *only* a matter of contrast. I didn't think it could be done quite this well, and I didn't want to try until I thought I'd worked out the problem."

"Well, you've straightened everything out splendidly. Congratulations."

Now he was visibly troubled. "But I didn't."

"Didn't what?"

"I didn't straighten everything out. It shouldn't work." Liao pondered the sky, which was laced with dark wisps of smoke that were rapidly fading out of sight as the breeze pulled them apart. "That is, of course it works—the rocketry and the incendiaries, I mean. And I know how to mix dark colors." He reached down and lifted a third rocket, turning it over in his hand. "But they shouldn't look quite as nice as they do. I expected us to be able to see them, but not like this." Almost reluctantly, he fitted the new firework into the stand and lit the fuse.

It burst overhead in a flowering of deep and velvety green, and it was as if a broad-leafed palm had suddenly sprouted in midair. For an emerald-spangled moment Lucy was transported back to a beach in Java where she had once lain under a sheltering tree and been surrounded by light very much like this.

"Obviously you solved the problem without realizing it," she said.

Liao shook his head. "No, I didn't."

Lucy frowned. "I don't understand."

He hesitated for a long moment, a small boy wrestling with some very great question. "Lucy, is there something different about me?"

"Different from before? Different how?"

"No, different from other people. Different from you."

"Well," Lucy remarked, hoping to lighten the suddenly heavy mood, "I expect you've noticed you're half Chinese."

"Not that." He reached for the end of his queue and worried it with his thumb and forefinger. "It was something Mr Blister said when we were making fireworks in his wagon."

"Mr. Blister said you were different?"

"He asked if I ever surprised myself with things I could do with fireworks. I said that I sometimes amazed other people, but not myself. He told me to try sometime—to try something I hadn't dared before. Something I didn't think would work, or perhaps something I might not even have thought was possible. Mr. Blister said I might surprise myself then. And when I asked why he supposed I might be able to do the impossible, he said, 'Because I believe you are special.'"

"Oh." Lucy considered. "I expect he meant you might know more than you think you do. You do things I should have thought were impossible all the time."

"But that's only because you don't know any better," Liao said. She snorted. "It isn't as if I'm doing magic," he explained. "I'm just doing things you didn't realize could be done." Liao tucked his knees up close to his chest. "He said, 'I believe you can do things other people can't. I think you are a salamander, like me.'"

"A salamander?" Lucy repeated. "One of those little lizard things?"

"No. Or yes, but he wasn't saying I was a lizard. It's folklore, like your coin under the mast. In folklore, salamanders are fire spirits. I've seen them as illustrations in fireworking formularies." He scratched at one palm with his finger. "It's like the cald-fire. You remember?"

"Of course I remember. But he told us how he did it. It isn't as if he were doing magic, either, Liao."

"No," Liao said slowly. "Not magic."

"He said there was a solution of some sort on his fingers, didn't he?"

Her brother's reply was quick and certain. "He was lying."

Lucy gaped at him. "Lying? Why on earth would he lie? And how do you know?"

"I know. The same way I know he wouldn't have put the cald-fire into your palm."

"He told you to snuff it out just as you were going to pass it to me," Lucy remembered.

Liao nodded. "I don't think you could have held it."

"But he could. And *you* could, because . . . ?"

"Because we are salamanders, I suppose."

"Salamanders," Lucy scoffed. "And what, exactly, is that supposed to mean? If you're a fire spirit, Liao, I'll eat my hat. You're my *brother*."

"I know. But I also know these rockets shouldn't work as well as they do." He sighed and lit the fourth, and over the river a starburst of deepest violet erupted, so that until it faded, night seemed to be slipping in through a million perfectly arranged slits in the curtain of bright blue sky.

"So . . . what are you saying, then? Do *you* think you're different somehow?"

Liao's reply was so quiet, Lucy had to ask him to speak up. He cast a sideways glance at her. "I said, I wonder if he somehow knows about my mother."

"About Jinna? Knows what?"

"But that doesn't make sense," Liao continued. "What I do isn't *tàiqīng*. It's not even *xiǎoshù*. It's not *wàidān* at all. It's just . . . just chemistry."

"I don't know what any of those words mean, Liao."

"Chemistry is to do with how, say, black powder reacts with—"

"I understand the meaning of *chemistry*. It's when you talk in break-teeth foreign words that I don't—"

"But the word *chemistry* comes from Arabic and Greek. It's just as foreign as—"

"Liao. Never mi—" She stopped, surprised. "Since when do you have Arabic and Greek?"

"We spent that week in the Levant, remember? Before we came to Nagspeake, and Mr. Harrick made friends with that Egyptian gunner."

"How much could you possibly have picked up from one

Egyptian gunner in a week? You called the holystone a blessed rock, for goodness' sake."

"Words come easy, so long as they mean things to do with incendiaries." They sat in the cutter for a long moment without speaking. "That's not normal, is it?" he asked at last.

"It's not *common,* I think," Lucy answered carefully. "But then, we knew you were never precisely common."

"No," Liao agreed, although he still sounded a bit disquieted. "No, I suppose we're neither of us precisely common."

"That's right." *But that's not quite true,* Lucy thought. *Ashore, I'm common. Ashore, I'm just like everyone else, except everyone else seems to manage without their heart breaking all the time.* She made her mouth up into a smile. "That's just exactly so, Liao."

Back in his room above the tavern, the rapping noise that Trigemine had been ignoring for some indeterminate length of time crescendoed to an insistent pounding. He got to his feet, blinking variables from his eyes and unable to let go of the threads of his calculations long enough to be properly annoyed at the interruption.

He flung open the door, then trooped back inside with Blister in tow. He ignored the peddler's questions and sat down at the table, which was littered with the tools that traveled with him: calipers, a set of Napier's Bones, a baize-covered box of many-sided dice carved from the bone and horn of a variety of creatures, a shagreen box that held a collection of lenses, and a small black globe on a silver stand. The sphere was covered in numbers and lines and symbols chalked in white and yellow and red. And, of course, there was the kairos mechanism itself, lying belly-up so that Trigemine could consult the spiral slide rule.

"I said, *well?*" Blister sounded exasperated. For all Trigemine was aware, he might have been repeating himself for the last hour.

"Do you want me to finish this or not?" Trigemine snarled without looking up. At least, he meant to snarl. In actuality, he was so intent on completing the work that the question came out in a mumble, and he wasn't entirely sure he'd finished the sentence. But it didn't matter. Just one more equation . . . maybe two . . .

Another few minutes or perhaps a few hours passed with Trigemine only vaguely aware of Blister's impatient pacing on the other side of the table. He finished computing a particularly knotty probability, double-checked his math, triple-checked it, then set down his pencil and stared at the result for a while. He checked his workings one last time, then picked up the pencil again and wrote out a second equation using the result from the first.

Then he drew the baize box closer and sifted his fingers through the contents until he found a die with so many sides that it resembled the faceted eye of an insect. The exterior was made from nearly transparent horn, and inside the hollow interior another die was nestled. Tucked within the translucent sides of *that* die was another, and within that, another still. Each was just small enough to move freely within the larger piece that enclosed it. Trigemine's unaided eye could see five nested dice, but there were more, and each side of each one was inscribed with finely etched markings.

He set the die reverently on the table and selected a lens from the shagreen box. Fitting it into his eye like a monocle, he took up the die once more. Instead of a single piece, he now saw a swarm of uncountable dice, a cloud of transparent horn and etchings that seemed to twine and slither, a mist of probability that drifted in his palm.

Trigemine closed his hand over it and shook. When he opened his hand to throw it on the table, what had been a single object once again became a fog that poured rather than fell to the surface and pooled there.

He positioned his pencil hand above a clean sheet of paper and leaned over the mist. Through the lens the haze cleared, resolving itself into a single faceted bit of horn. The lens also magnified the die enough for Trigemine's eye to identify the uppermost side, and to find the constellation of dots engraved there. Without looking away, he drew the constellation on the fresh paper. Then he gazed deeper, to the uppermost facet of the next die and the symbol cut into it. Moving his hand just slightly, he drew that symbol below the dots, then he refocused his eyes so the symbol and the dots became a single image, and Trigemine drew that. He blinked and stared until he found the polygon engraved on the die two layers in, drew that, and drew the image formed by the polygon, the symbol, and the dots. He blinked again, sought out the uppermost facet of the die four layers in, and repeated the process.

He repeated it. And repeated it. And repeated it.

His eyeballs were red and aching before he finally sat back and popped out the lens. Trigemine dropped his pencil, closed his eyes, and rubbed his temples with the heels of his hands. Then he raised his gaze at last and nearly jumped out of his skull to find Blister sitting across the table, glowering and furious.

"How long have you been there?" Trigemine demanded.

"Hours!" the peddler exploded.

"Is that all?" Trigemine cracked his neck and glanced at the window. The afternoon sky was gone, and now a curtain of night hung outside the glass.

He turned his attention back to the table and reached for the paper. On one side of the page was the column of individual etchings from each nested die. On the other side was the column that showed the progress of a single, combined image that had grown, layer by layer, as Trigemine had peered deeper and deeper into the die. He reached for the black spherical chalkboard, wiped it clean with spit and his own sleeve, and copied onto it the composite image from the very bottom of that column, labeling its various sides and angles with numbers from the collection of equations he'd worked out beforehand.

At length, he sat back. "Blister," he said slowly, "I'm going to tell you some things you're going to think are crazy."

"About time!"

Trigemine ignored the outburst. His eyes landed on a coil of silver cord slung over the back of Blister's chair. "I take it you found what you went for?"

"I did." Blister patted the cord. "I knew we'd have no problem on that front. I was owed a favor."

"A favor? By whom?"

"By Forgeron, of course."

Trigemine went white. "The fellow Swifte's staying with? That's where you went for your miraculous cable?"

"Of course. You don't think the sort of cord that can at least theoretically bind a minor deity is something any old metalsmith can whip up in a morning, do you? But don't worry. I made certain your Ironmonger wasn't in. Forgeron owes me several rather large debts. He won't speak of my visit, and I didn't speak of your business with Swifte."

"And you didn't think to tell me there was another person involved in your preparations *before I did all this?*" He waved at the mess of tools and workings.

"But I did!" Blister snapped his fingers. "Oh, perhaps I told you his proper name! Forgero. isn't his real one, of course."

Riffling through pages of calculations, Trigemine found his original notes. "Cassiterides Bone."

"That's him."

Trigemine dropped the notebook and pinched the bridge of his nose. "Well, mercifully, at least the reckonings should stand, then. I don't think I have another round in me."

"And so?"

"There's a way we can take the boy, his mother, and the Albatross all at once. The key is the girl."

"The girl?"

"The boy's sister."

"I barely noticed her."

"Then you're not very observant." Trigemine thought back

to the long moments outside Blister's wagon with the wary Lucy Bluecrowne. What his reckonings seemed to suggest she could accomplish . . . And yet, he'd double- and triple-checked everything at every stage until the moment he'd rolled the fly's-eye die, which was the final step and the only one that couldn't be done over. The Bluecrowne girl was evidently a more formidable force than either of them had suspected.

All that remained was to apply that force correctly, and the girl would bring them a conflagrationeer, a reliquary, and a weapon. "When it comes time, Blister, will you be able to best this Lady Xiaoming?"

The peddler's face creased into a grim smile. He patted the silver coil. "I think so, though there will be some . . . some fireworks, shall we say. We'll need a place to work. Somewhere we won't be remarked. But I know a spot."

"Good. Excellent." Trigemine smiled too, then passed out cold on the tabletop.

TEN

A THUMPING GREAT BLUE

"**O**UT *or down! Out or down! Here I come with a sharp knife and a clear conscience!*"

Lucy bolted upright in her hammock and swung her legs over the side. If she'd been operating on anything more than instinct, she might have remembered where she was and that one of the supposed benefits of shore-going life was that there were no watches for which to report. Therefore, there ought to be no one coming with a sharp knife to cut down the hammocks of any oversleepers.

"*Out or down, Lucy!*"

She might also have realized that the voice bellowing in her ear sounded suspiciously like a small boy's. But it was such a relief to hear the familiar shout that her sleeping body was out and on its feet before her eyes were even properly open. She discovered that she was blinking blearily at a grinning Liao—who did, rather disturbingly, have an open knife in one hand. They eyed each other for a moment.

"You weren't actually going to cut down my hammock, were you, you little monster?" Lucy asked.

Liao folded the blade closed and slipped it nonchalantly into his pocket. "Certainly not," he answered, all innocence.

"No, I thought as much." Without a doubt, they were both lying. "What time is it?"

"What does it matter? Today is the day, Lucy," Liao sang. "The day of the blue of the *world!*"

"It matters quite a lot if you were about to cut my hammock lines." Lucy jabbed a finger at the door. "Out, while I dress. Your peddlers aren't coming for hours yet. Pipe down."

Liao, however, singularly failed to pipe himself down and was all but bouncing off the walls when she emerged. They ran to the kitchen and followed the sound of the steward humming "Roast Beef of Old England" in the pantry. "Good morning, Garvett," Lucy called.

Garvett emerged and touched his knuckles to his forehead in salute. "Morning, miss. Sir."

"Morning!" Liao returned the salute and clambered up onto a stool beside the big table, where he took a scone from a basket. Then he went scurrying out again, shouting something over his shoulder about getting the workshop shipshape.

"I thought I ought to help you with breakfast," Lucy said, surveying the kitchen without a clue as to how one might do such a thing. "Might I lend a hand?"

Garvett's eyebrows twitched up toward his hairline. "Lend a hand? With breakfast?" he asked with a faintly offended air. "Miss Bluecrowne, I know I ain't Cook, but begging your pardon, if I weren't equal to the task of feeding this little household, I'm not sure how much you'd change the state of things. Begging your pardon, miss."

"I could make the tea," Lucy offered, pointing to the one object she recognized. It was impossible to mistake a kettle, and she was fairly certain all you had to do to get the process started was add water.

Garvett narrowed his eyes and did something with his tongue behind his lips. "Aye, tea you likely could manage with a try or two." He twitched his chin at a cask beside the kitchen door. "The water in the scuttlebutt's fresh. Mind the stove, now—it's hot."

Lucy glowered. Every man jack aboard the *Left-Handed Fate* had come to accept a seven-year-old boy playing with fire and worse, but evidently she, at twelve, could not be trusted to put a teakettle on the stove without harming herself. Then she remembered why she had offered to help with breakfast in the first place and forced a smile. "I will. Thank you, Garvett." She carried the pot to the scuttlebutt and ladled water into it.

The steward eyed the dipper dripping onto the floor. "Never known you to be curious about galley work," he observed as he piled raw chops on a plate.

"Well, I haven't got much else to do," Lucy said as she plunked the kettle on the stove. Then she realized that might sound insulting. "Excuse me."

He grinned. "Not to worry, miss. We're in the same boat, you and I. I hope you won't mind if I say I'd much rather be aboard ship too."

"No, I don't mind." She watched the teakettle, willing it to boil faster. "Garvett, could I ask a favor of you?"

"Ah. Now we come to it." He wiped his hands and folded his arms. "What is it, then?"

"Could you show me how to bake some small cakes? In time for dinner?"

"Cakes," he repeated warily.

"Little ones," Lucy said quickly. "Nothing fancy like a pudding. I know that takes ages."

"But *you* want to bake these cakes?"

Not really, she didn't. The tea-making alone was boring Lucy to tears. Still. "I need to pack a basket to trade today for some powders and things for Liao. I thought it would be easy enough to make up some cold beef and maybe what's left of last night's sea-pie, but the peddler specifically asked for cakes. And seven-water grog."

"*Nobody* wants seven-water grog," Garvett retorted, his eyes narrowing as if this was further evidence—Lucy's wish to cook at all being the first—that she was making some sort of game of him.

"Well, he asked Liao what he likes to drink," Lucy explained. "I think he means to share."

"Oh." The steward rubbed his chin. "And when is this trade meant to happen, then?"

"The peddler's coming by at two bells in the afternoon watch," Lucy answered as the kettle began whistling.

Garvett grabbed for her elbow and missed. "Belay there, don't—"

The warning wasn't quite quick enough. In her haste to prove that she could manage in a kitchen, Lucy leapt for the kettle and completely forgot to wonder whether the handle might be hot before she grabbed it. The handle, in fact, was *scorching*.

"Nackle-arsed sonofabitch!" She flung it away and cradled her hand to her chest. "Blood and eyes!"

The kettle fell with a clatter, rolling clumsily and flinging boiling water in all directions before disappearing under the stove. Lucy and Garvett looked at the steaming runnels of water collecting in the spaces between the red tiles, and then at each other.

"I could just go to the Harbors and buy some cakes, if you think that's simpler," Lucy said at last.

"Give us your palm," Garvett ordered. She shook out her hand, which was starting to ache quite a lot, and put it into the steward's. Garvett examined with a critical eye the oblong white welt that was forming there. "There's a bottle or two of the captain's good champagne in the springhouse. Go and hold the neck of a bottle against the burn and keep the whole in the spring. Stay there until I send for you. Then a bit of oil to dress it and you'll be right as rain. Except for the pain," he added as an afterthought. "But then, you can manage a bit of pain, I imagine."

"Certainly I can, but—"

Garvett sniffed. "Cook would never let me hear the end of it if I sent you off to market for something simple as a bit of dessert. Old bastard already thinks I'm like to starve you all without him here to tell me how to light the stove. And you ain't to tell him about this matter of the kettle, either," he said severely. "Not a word of it, miss, do you hear?"

"Yes, Garvett," Lucy said meekly. "And . . . you won't tell Papa about what I said, will you? During the . . . the matter of the kettle?"

"Begging your pardon, miss, but don't be a bloody idiot." He pointed sharply at the kitchen door. "Springhouse. Off with you."

Garvett left her out there to soak her hand until after seven bells. Lucy sat and endured her punishment with her aching hand wrapped around one of the cold bottles of champagne submerged in the little spring that bubbled up out of the rock. "I hate being ashore," she groaned.

In the end, it was Liao who bounded in to summon her back to the house. "Cousin Nellie and Papa have arrived in the launch, and Mr. Garvett says you may come in now for your olive oil," Liao announced. He held out an empty jug. "And he says will you please fill this for mixing the grog."

Lucy brightened as she took the jug with her good hand and dunked it in the spring. "Nellie's here?" Nell Levinflash was a sort of honorary cousin to Lucy and Liao. She was an official on the staff of the Quartermaster, the head of Nagspeake's Flotilla district, but for a brief time, Nell had been a master's mate aboard the *Left-Handed Fate,* and Mr. Wooll, the sailing master, still spoke of her as the most brilliant navigator he'd ever known.

"Yes, she is. Did you really burn yourself making *tea?*"

"I suppose you know how to make tea," she groused.

"Of course I do," Liao laughed. "And I brought you some of my mother's salve for the burn. I have it here." He patted his pocket, then lowered his voice. "Best let Garvett use the olive oil first."

Lucy nodded forcefully. Hell had no fury like a seaman—particularly a steward—whose preferred remedies were disdained.

They returned to the house, Liao talking all the way about the peddler's forthcoming visit and how afterward he would certainly help Lucy with the cutter if she wished, and how he would put together a very special rocket with the new capital blue he was about to learn so that they might celebrate the boat's first official voyage, and how clever Mr. Blister was and how good Lucy was to make up a dinner basket even though Garvett had already done everything but the cakes and the grog, and did Lucy really think Mr. Blister would prefer cakes to plain crunchy ship's biscuit that he might dunk in a cup of chocolate? Mr. Blister might not have ever sampled the ambrosia that was ship's biscuit, or experienced the excellent fun that was knocking live weevils out of it before one dunked it in a cup of chocolate and ate it up in exactly four bites.

In the kitchen, Lucy presented her hand to be dressed with olive oil and wrapped in a linen bandage. Then she and Liao crept past the adult voices in the parlor and went upstairs, where they unwrapped the bandage again so that Liao could daub the burn with a pinkish salve from the little painted ceramic jar in his pocket. The ache of the forming blister dulled immediately. They rewrapped the linen as well as they could and headed back downstairs just as Kendrick began ringing eight bongs on the ship's bell outside the front door.

Then Lucy stopped short. Someone in the dining room had

just said her name. She waved Liao back and the two of them crouched on the stairs.

"Will you really leave her here?" It was Nellie's voice. "She will wither, sir."

"You didn't," Lucy's father countered.

"That's different. I chose it, staying ashore, because in the end, this city means even more to me than the sea. Nagspeake *is* my ship. But *nothing* means more to Lucy than the sea, except perhaps you and that tub you call a schooner."

"If you had seen that gash, Nell . . ."

There was a small sigh. "Her heart is an albatross, Captain: the size of an eagle and tied to the oceans. It will break. She won't survive on land."

"She's not so weak as that," Lucy's father protested. "On land or on sea, she's strong. She's the strongest creature I've ever seen."

"A shark's strong too, but if you cast it on the shore—hell, if it so much as stops swimming—it dies."

"Enough." That was Xiaoming. "The two of you will have plenty of time to discuss this in Flotilla."

Plates clattered and Garvett's voice mumbled something about the chops. Lucy hesitated a moment more, composing herself, then she and Liao joined the group in the dining room. There she found her father, standing with a cup and saucer in one hand in a posture that suggested he might have been pacing a moment before. Sitting on opposite sides of the table were Xiaoming and another tall and dark-haired young woman.

"Lucy!" Nell threw her arms open, and Lucy hugged her tightly.

Thank you for what you said, she wanted to whisper. *Thank you for knowing my heart.* Instead, she poured all her gratitude into the embrace. From the way Nell hugged her back, Lucy suspected that the older girl knew what she wanted to say, even without speaking.

"How comes the cutter, Lucy?" Captain Bluecrowne asked as they all sat down.

"Very well, sir. This afternoon I'll begin caulking."

"We took her out yesterday," Liao added.

"And Liao set off some fireworks that —" Lucy paused. Across the table, Liao's smile became brittle. He shook his head just a fraction.

"That what?" Xiaoming asked in a tone that held something more than just curiosity. Liao plucked a bit of pickled radish from a bowl on the table and jammed it in his mouth to avoid having to answer. He flashed Lucy a panicked glance as he chewed.

"That weren't too much to upset the barky," Lucy finished. "There's space right in the bow for him to send up rockets to his heart's delight."

Liao nodded rapidly. His mother gave him a long look, then turned to her plate. Lucy waited for Liao's eyes to come back to hers, but he only asked for the bread barge to be passed his way. He scowled into it when it arrived, then reluctantly took a piece of fresh bread and dunked it in his chocolate.

"Well, that's good news. Have you everything you need for the next few days, then?" the captain inquired.

"I think so, Papa. Why?"

"Nell's been good enough to arrange to have the hull re-coppered, but we shall have to take the *Fate* to Flotilla today."

Lucy lowered her toast. "Today?" Flotilla was down the river in Nagspeake proper, about halfway between the Quayside Harbors and the Atlantic, but it might as well have been Java as far as Lucy was concerned. While the *Fate* was docked in the Harbors, Lucy could get to her in less than an hour. In Flotilla she was all but out of reach. Panic bubbled up in her throat. *They can't leave yet! Not even for a few days!* "When?" she asked as evenly as she could manage.

"We weigh anchor at two bells of the afternoon watch. I tell you what it is, Lucy. This is the best fellow in Nagspeake for this sort of work, and Nell's pulled all sorts of strings to get him to shift his schedule for us."

Lucy's heart sank all the way down to her knees. Of course there was no missing an opportunity to have the hull re-coppered. Scraping away the seaweed and barnacles the schooner had been trailing for months would help her speed, but a new copper belly was even better. Still, now her father and her vessel would spend much of their remaining time in Nagspeake too far away for her to visit.

She became aware that everyone at the table was looking at her with sympathy. Nell's face, in particular, was all heartbreak. *I'm sorry,* she mouthed silently.

"I understand you and Liao have plans for the afternoon," Xiaoming said gently. "I am going down to the *Fate* with your father and Miss Levinflash. Is there anything I might bring back for you?"

Liao shifted in his chair. Lucy could see what he was thinking. He was going to try to convince her to forget their plans and spend the day aboard ship instead.

Her heart jumped. Garvett could finish the peddlers' dinner, and Liao certainly didn't need Lucy there to supervise him with explosives, not when she couldn't be trusted with so much as a hot teakettle. If she went with her father now, and if the schooner wasn't meant to leave before one, she would have a good three hours aboard the *Fate* before it left the Quayside Harbors.

But no, she decided abruptly, it wouldn't do. If she couldn't let the *Fate* go now, she would never survive when it left for good. Worse, she would be shirking a duty, even if that duty was nothing more than a matter of cakes and grog.

"Lucy," Liao began, "should you not perhaps —"

"Yes," Lucy interrupted, turning to Xiaoming. "Yes, Jìmǔ, you could do me a kindness, if you would. Please excuse me."

She rushed from the dining room and up the stairs to the floor above, wiping dampness from her cheeks. On her desk was the slip of paper upon which Liao had written his Chinese translation of their surname. Lucy grabbed a page of her new stationery and scrawled three sentences on it, then folded the page around the smaller bit of paper and tied the whole thing closed with string. She took a few deep breaths and touched her cheeks to make certain there was no lingering evidence of sadness there, and then she headed back down to the dining room.

"Would you be so kind as to give this to the armorer aboard ship?" she asked, handing the little parcel to Xiaoming. "And if you please, ma'am, it would be best if you didn't peek."

She glanced at Liao, realizing a moment too late that she should have asked him before changing the plan. He gave Lucy a conspiratorial wink. "Yes, please," he said to his mother.

Xiaoming took the parcel carefully. "As you wish."

"Well, this is exciting!" Blister announced as he and Trigemine hiked up the last few of what seemed like several thousand steps to the top of the cliff. "And isn't that *something?*"

"Hmm?" Trigemine was accustomed to long marches over far more forbidding terrain, so although his legs were aching and his lungs were working hard, he'd had enough energy left to spend the interminable hike going over the reckonings he had done the night before. He'd gotten good and lost in his own head, to the extent that he'd nearly forgotten the other man was there.

He roused himself from his mathematical thoughts and noticed for the first time the house that stood before them. "Good lord." It *was* something. In all his wanderings, Trigemine had never seen anything quite like it. It hardly seemed to belong to either the here or the now, but even he couldn't figure where or when it might fit.

Blister set the bag he had been carrying on the landing at his feet and wiped a thin sheen of sweat from his nose with an embroidered handkerchief. "Perhaps this is what passes for a palace if one is a privateer."

"*Letter-of-marque,*" Trigemine said. "I am told they prefer *letter-of-marque.*"

"Yes, thank you." Blister slung his bag of goods over his shoulder once more. "Ready, friend?"

"Lead on."

They had just reached the portico and Trigemine was in the process of lifting his hand to the bronze knocker when the door swung inward and Liao Bluecrowne came bounding out. "They have arrived, they have arrived!" he crowed, dancing around Blister as if he were a maypole.

"We have, indeed!" Blister sounded as excited as Liao.

The girl, Lucy, appeared in the doorway. She gave them a civil nod and waved a hand inside. "Should you like to come in and rest after the hike up?"

"Not a bit of it!" Blister winked. "Provided there's a dinner basket packed and ready. No sense wasting time when there are fireworks to be made."

"Certainly," she replied. "If you or Mr. Trigemine will be so kind as to carry it, it's just here."

"With seven-water grog?" Blister asked, mock-severe. "And cake?"

Liao nodded feverishly. "Lucy baked the cakes herself!"

Trigemine touched his hat and made a short bow. "Allow me. I'm not likely to be useful for much else." The basket sat just next to the door. Lucy stepped aside to allow Trigemine to enter, and he saw something, some momentary hesitation flicker over her face as he bent to pick it up. Distrust? Or just curiosity? *What does she think she senses?* he wondered.

"That's quite a nice pin," Lucy said, looking at his cravat. "I noticed it back in the Harbors."

"Thank you." Trigemine straightened. "I use it to walk through time." And with that, he took the basket and followed Blister and Liao to a stone outbuilding across the lawn, leaving Lucy Bluecrowne to look after him in confusion.

They were already inside and having a disagreement when he reached the door of the stone building. "But I know how to make stars," Liao protested.

"All the better. You mustn't be distracted by the making of some fanciful compound firework. The blue on its own is complex enough. So we shall make it up in a batch of rolled stars."

"Where shall I put this?" Trigemine asked, shifting the burden in his arms and glancing around the small space. At the back stood an orderly assemblage of casks and crates, some of the latter of which had been opened and unpacked onto the shelves that lined the upper halves of every wall but the one with the door. The shelves were pitted with age, but the two long workbenches on either side below them looked new-built.

"Oh, anyplace at all." Liao was plainly dying to get started.

"But first, a toast," Blister suggested. "Where is that famous grog?"

Trigemine set the basket down on the bench to his left and undid its latch. Between two cloth-wrapped bundles, there was a speckled earthenware jug and a pair of tin cups tucked inside. "I imagine this is what we're after."

"Splendid." Blister took the jug and poured a measure into each cup, then glanced sharply at Trigemine. Trigemine, in turn, glanced over his shoulder to be sure Lucy Bluecrowne wasn't standing directly behind him. His comment about walking through time had thrown her, just as he'd hoped, and she was only now making her way across the grounds. Liao, meanwhile, was busy rooting through a rattling crate of metal molds, presumably looking for one appropriate for making the stars Blister had insisted they begin with.

Blister reached into his vest pocket, produced a vial, and tipped the contents into one of the cups. Trigemine gave it a swish, and glittering emerald flecks swirled and disappeared. Then Blister took both cups from Trigemine, turned, and handed one to the boy. "To a thumping great blue."

Trigemine stepped out into the daylight. Lucy Bluecrowne was halfway across the lawn now. He put his hand into his watch pocket and counted to five. As the world dissolved around him, the workshop at his back exploded. He felt it as a vague heat and a sharp push like the force of a sudden, rough wind, but that was all.

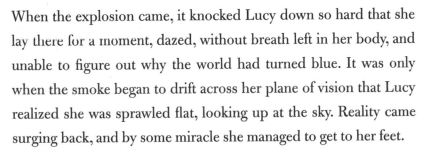

When the explosion came, it knocked Lucy down so hard that she lay there for a moment, dazed, without breath left in her body, and unable to figure out why the world had turned blue. It was only when the smoke began to drift across her plane of vision that Lucy realized she was sprawled flat, looking up at the sky. Reality came surging back, and by some miracle she managed to get to her feet.

She stumbled toward the smoking, shattered pile of rubble

that was all that remained of her brother's workshop. *"Liao!"* She knew she was screaming, could feel the scream ripping itself from her throat, but she could hear nothing but an angry buzz. Still, she screamed her brother's name the whole way across the great lawn, and by the time strong hands wrestled her to the ground only a few yards from the smoldering wood and broken stone and her hearing had begun to come back, her voice had gone completely.

"Stay here," Kendrick ordered, and from where she lay, held down with her cheek against the grass, Lucy watched helplessly as he sprinted into the wreckage.

"Let me up," she sobbed. The hands that had been restraining her pulled her upright and embraced her tightly.

"You mustn't go, miss." It was Garvett's voice this time.

"Liao is in there!"

"Kendrick's gone for him, Miss Bluecrowne, and if you'll stay back, I'll go too." He hugged her tighter. "Say you'll stay back, Lucy. Will you stay here?"

"Turn me loose, Garvett!"

"Will you stay?" Garvett shouted directly in her face, shaking her hard. Lucy shook her head no but heard herself cry *yes,* and the steward shoved her aside and ran after Kendrick. Lucy dropped to her knees in the grass.

A stone cup that Lucy recognized as Liao's favorite grinding mortar lay a few feet away. Its smooth quartz-flecked side was cracked from lip to base. Could it still be used, cracked like that? Would it break clean in half when it was picked up? *He'll regret losing that mortar extremely,* she thought helplessly.

Farther away, Garvett's blurry shape plunged into the hole where the door to the workshop had been, and for a moment both he and the half-demolished outbuilding dissolved into ripples. Lucy wiped the tears and dirt from her eyes with her sleeve, and the world regained some of its sharpness. She counted to three.

Garvett appeared from around the back of the building. There had been no door at the back of the workshop before the blast. He didn't look at Lucy, just headed deeper into the woods. His head swept from side to side. He was looking at the ground. Then Kendrick's big figure appeared in the blasted-out doorway. His eyes fell on Lucy. His face was as pale as milk. The world dissolved into watercolor again, and Lucy let out a moan.

Kendrick knelt beside her and picked her up with shaking hands. Lucy had never seen the coxswain's hands shake before. She hadn't known they could. She licked her lips and tasted earth and grass and gunpowder. "Where is he?" she managed.

Because he had not come out, he must still be inside, and the only reason she could think of that he would still be inside was that he couldn't come out on his own. But if that had been the case, surely Kendrick would've carried him out and they would all be rushing him into the house now to clap bandages on, and Garvett would've run for the river to find a surgeon instead of into the woods for whatever reason.

"Has he . . ." Lucy licked her lips again. "Has he lost the number of his mess?" Which was the closest she could come to asking, *Is he dead?*

"He's gone, Lucy," Kendrick whispered in a strange tone, and

Lucy's heart died in her chest and she felt her legs sway beneath her. "No, no," he added quickly, squeezing her against his side so that she wouldn't fall. "No, love, I mean he simply isn't to be found. Bear up, now, that's a good girl."

"He isn't to be found?" There was nothing simple about that. Liao had been in the building, and then the building had exploded. "Where else could he be?"

"I don't know, but there's no sign of him. Which is a sight better than a body, now, isn't it?" Kendrick's eyes flitted around, searching. "The peddlers?"

"What?"

"The powder merchants, Lucy. Were they in the workshop when—"

"I don't . . ." Lucy forced herself to think. It was hard. It hurt her aching head. "One was inside, with . . ." She swallowed. "The other . . . I can't remember."

Kendrick shook his head fractionally. "It doesn't matter. Go inside the house now."

"Kendrick. If he . . ." *If he blew himself up at last . . .* ". . . then there wouldn't be a . . ." *A body.*

Kendrick hesitated. "There would be . . . signs. We should be able to tell, Lucy."

Of course. Bodies left traces. How often had she seen those smatterings aboard the *Fate* after a battle? Her stomach clenched, and she felt its contents surge upward as she imagined bits of Liao spattered across the lawn. But Kendrick had said there were no such traces to be seen, and she managed to swallow it all down again. "Then where—what—" She beat her fists against her fore-head. *"Where is Liao?"*

"I don't know. He may have been hurt and wandered into the woods without his wits quite about him. That does happen when one takes a blow, sometimes." Kendrick let her go carefully. "Best I get after Garvett and help search. If Liao hasn't got his wits about him, he may do himself a mischief or wander off the cliff. Go inside, Lucy. Go inside and wait."

He stayed until she stammered her agreement, then he turned and took off at a run for the trees, leaving Lucy to make her way back to the porch on jellied legs. She wandered through the open door and lowered herself carefully into one of the chairs in the par-lor. She sat numbly, staring at the cold, empty fireplace, seeing noth-ing and trying hard not to think.

"They won't find him, you know."

The voice was calm, utterly soothing—so soothing, Lucy al-most didn't realize what the kind words were actually saying. She turned and found the tall peddler called Trigemine silhouetted in the doorway, regarding her with his hands clasped before him.

"They might," she said dully. "He isn't in the wreckage, Kend-rick says. He might still be alive."

"He's alive, yes," Trigemine said gently, "but he's gone as surely as if he'd been blown to pieces and those pieces scattered to the four winds." Lucy sucked in a breath, horrified at the words being uttered with so much sympathy by this man whose eyes were so bright and cold. "Blister has him now," he continued. "They won't find him."

Lucy stared at Trigemine, uncomprehending. Then his meaning pierced her shock, and she launched herself to her feet. "Blister has taken him away?"

Trigemine nodded slowly.

"Taken him to safety, you mean? From the explosion?"

"That is not what I mean, no. He has taken Liao for his own reasons."

"But he's alive?"

He inclined his head once more. "For all the good that does you. He's out of your reach."

"Where is he?"

"Now, don't be foolish. Why would I tell you that?"

"Because—because —" It was as if her mind were full of treacle and all the mechanisms that allowed her to think were gummed up and turning far too slowly. Of course he wouldn't tell. "You're in league with him."

"Obviously."

"Where is my brother?" Where were her wits? Where were the razor-sharp reflexes that had carried her through battles at sea? Why could she not find them now, with her enemy standing perfectly still before her?

Rutting land.

"Liao is gone, Lucy. Gone for good." Trigemine strode across the parlor and looked at her with deep concern. "Blister came to Nagspeake to find him, and very soon he will leave with the boy and that will be the end of it. Liao will be gone from your life forever."

"Why are you telling me this?" she asked in a whisper, sinking back into her chair.

"Because I can get him back for you." He reached across the space between them and took one of Lucy's shaking hands. His fingers curled protectively around her bandaged palm even as his icy blue eyes pinned her like a caught beetle. "Or, more accurately, I can give you what you need to get him back. Would you like that?"

Even through her shock and fear, Lucy knew enough to be certain she didn't like *anything* about this. Still, if Liao was alive, there was only one possible answer for her to give. "Tell me how."

Trigemine's lips shifted into a smile. "There is a man with a knife. He's called Christopher Swifte. Get me his knife and you'll have your brother back. The boy for the knife. I'll even give you the boy first. Straightforward enough for you?"

"You'll give Liao back first? Why would you do that?"

"Because while I want to help Blister, I want the knife more. And, properly speaking, I'm not just going to hand the boy over. I'm going to tell you where he is. Then you and your privateer mates—I'm sorry, your *letter-of-marque* mates—will be welcome to pop in and take him."

"Then what's to —"

"If you turn up there without the knife—or if anyone else turns up before you do—I'll whisk Blister and Liao away faster than you can blink." Trigemine flicked his coat open and reached into the watch pocket of his vest. "Away, and out of your reach forever. And this is what it will look like."

And then he vanished.

Lucy lurched out of her chair again and turned in a circle,

searching the room. She was, suddenly and impossibly, completely alone. She could feel the emptiness of the house around her.

"Is it a bargain?" With no more warning than when he'd disappeared, Trigemine stood before her, gazing down with those brutally frigid eyes.

It was a bad bargain. It had to be. Moreover, why Liao? She very nearly asked what Blister wanted with him, then remembered what her brother had said the day before aboard the *Driven Star*. *When I asked why he supposed I might be able to do the impossible, he said, "Because I believe you are special."*

She opened her mouth to ask *why* Liao was special, but then she decided she didn't want to give Trigemine the satisfaction. "Why can't you get the knife yourself?" she demanded instead.

"Because Swifte won't sell it to me," he said patiently.

"So you need me to steal it."

Trigemine waved a hand. "If you can convince him to give it to you, by all means, do that. Simpler for all concerned, and not as impossible as it sounds. But I wouldn't make that your only plan of attack."

Lucy glanced over his shoulder and through the open front door, wishing Kendrick and Garvett would appear and take charge of this situation. But they were somewhere in the woods, somewhere out of sight, searching for Liao where, according to Trigemine, he was not. And Lucy had no doubt that Trigemine was telling the truth.

"Time is wasting, Lucy," the peddler said softly. "There is a moment for accomplishing impossible tasks, and that moment won't wait for you."

"All right," she said at last, standing as straight as she could manage. "Show me where to find my brother."

Trigemine put one hand on her shoulder and drew her to a window facing the Skidwrack. Through the trees on the opposite shore, sunlight glinted on glass. "That is a house, and that is where Blister will take your brother." Even as he spoke, a small boat pulled into view, sliding across the river to the far bank. Lucy pressed her hands to the pane, straining to make out any details, desperate to spot the small shape of her brother, but the vessel was nothing but a dark wedge on the water.

She swallowed hard and faced Trigemine. "Tell me where I may find this man and his knife, then."

ELEVEN

HOLLOWARE ROW

IT'S down to you and me," Lucy whispered as she leapt aboard the *Driven Star*.

She'd scrawled a hasty note for Kendrick and Garvett, but she hadn't wanted to be caught in the house when they came back. That would mean explaining where she was going and why, and if it got to that point, Lucy knew the sailors would insist on going straight away to try to rescue Liao themselves. After Trigemine's disappearing trick, to say nothing of the explosion that had destroyed the workshop but had evidently not hurt Blister and Liao, Lucy was sure it would be a bad idea to disobey the instructions she'd been given. When one was up against men who could disappear and blow up things without taking a scratch, what was there to do but precisely what they said?

She gave the cutter a quick looking-over to be sure everything was all a-tanto, then she cast off. For a moment, the world felt so normal that it actually hurt.

This was how she'd learned to sail: on a river very like this one and in a boat about this size. For a moment, Lucy allowed herself to imagine that when she reached the Harbors her father and the *Fate* would be there waiting, just as they had been the day she had sailed that first boat up a different river and back—and that this time, Liao would be there too. But only for a moment.

Thankfully, the Skidwrack didn't toss any surprises her way, and the *Driven Star* responded to Lucy's demands as if the barky understood the urgency. A quarter of an hour later she brought the cutter in at the far end of the Quayside Harbors. Here two small piers met the shore at a mossy, half-submerged flight of stairs alongside a crumbling bulkhead eaten away by age and water. Lucy fended the cutter off the bulkhead and tied her up to the decomposing wood. Then, grabbing her ditty bag and slinging it over one shoulder, she hurried up the slick steps and onto dry land.

This part of the Harbors appeared just as derelict as the rotting berth where she'd left her boat, but clearly it had once been a busy artisans' quarter. The abandoned workshops on all sides had expensively large glass panes in their darkened windows, and the shingles over the doors were elaborately carved, though their colors had gone dark with age and grime long ago. A sign half-drowned in cattails poked out of the reeds beside the road: FORNAX STREET.

Trying to ignore prickles of unease, Lucy hiked inland, passing more uninhabited and overgrown lanes: Tinplate Street, Tuyere Street, Bloomery Street. Then came one that was narrower and darker than the rest. Lucy read the fingerpost aloud, just to hear the sound of her voice and break the silence. "Holloware Row."

She turned, and Holloware Row led her past more grimy windows and more shingles with words made illegible by cloaks of cobwebs. Then she spotted a sign that was a touch brighter than the rest, as if someone had scrubbed it at least once in the last half-century. Beneath it a big dun mare stood, twitching her ears and chewing on the grasses that peeked up from in between the paving stones. Through the shadows, just enough light fell upon the shingle for Lucy to read the words JONAS FORGERON, CHAINWRIGHT. The windows of this workshop were dark too, but when she crept closer she discovered that they, unlike the others she'd passed, were hung with thick black curtains.

This was the place. As she eyed the door and the horse, Lucy remembered she had no plan for actually stealing the knife. She'd rushed to the boat, and then she'd had to focus on getting down the river, and now here she was with no idea of how to break in and take what she needed. She hadn't even brought any weapons, other than the work knife she always carried in her bag.

Well, she thought, *I do know something about slipping into a place and making off with something that isn't one's own.* Sailors called such an errand a cutting-out expedition, and Lucy had been on—or at least, had been in some way a party to—dozens of those. So if she were to approach the mission as something like a cutting-out . . .

Her eyes darted around the lane. Wheels began to turn. And then, oh, *and then,* a completely unexpected flood of wild joy swept over her, and she felt her mouth stretch into a grin. *Not* like *one,* she realized. *This* is *a cutting-out expedition.*

And with that, suddenly, for the first time in longer than she could recall, she remembered what it felt like to be the Lucy Bluecrowne she knew herself to be. It was a feeling like a freshening wind coming into becalmed sails, a feeling she had not believed she could ever have on land, because it had seemed achingly clear that *that* Lucy could not possibly exist ashore. And yet . . .

She scooted farther into the shadows and contemplated how her father went about planning a cutting-out. The *Left-Handed Fate* was a small vessel, so she could rarely rely on firepower to carry the day. But more than once, her father had taken the *Fate* or one of her even smaller boats into a harbor and cut out prize-ships without firing a single shot. Smaller, faster, cleverer—that was the *Left-Handed Fate,* and that was how she always won. *I shall simply have to be small, fast, and clever too,* Lucy decided.

The breeze in her sails strengthened, and she leaned out of the shadows and took another look around the street. Perhaps, she thought, eyeing the shingle opposite the chainwright's shop, if she could cut the rope that suspended the sign, the noise of its fall would bring Christopher Swifte out to investigate.

The shingle was held by moldering cordage that would certainly give Lucy's little knife no trouble, and the sign looked heavy enough to make a proper racket when it hit. But if it did manage to draw Swifte out-of-doors, it wouldn't keep him there long. No, she needed a plan that would buy her some time to search for the knife Trigemine had called the Albatross.

Her eyes fell on the horse. Now, there was a diversion with some potential. The mare was cropping weeds only a few feet from where that shingle would land when it fell. And, as Lucy understood it, horses generally did not care for sudden crashes.

Next, to make sure there was a way *in* while Christopher Swifte was out. The windows along the side of the building were low and hinged so that they could yawn wide into the passage between Forgeron's shop and its neighbor. Creeping along toward the back, Lucy found one with a cracked pane. It wasn't broken all the way through, but it was compromised enough that a sharp blow might do the rest of the job. With that pane gone, Lucy would be able to open the window from outside.

She returned to where the passage gave onto Holloware Row. Keeping low and whispering what she hoped were comforting things to the bay mare, Lucy crept up to the hitching post, untied the reins, and, stretching up on tiptoe, lifted them over the mare's head and laid them on her neck. Then she spat on her fingers and faced the brick front of the shop across the lane.

After spending her entire childhood climbing the rigging of a schooner flying over the water at fifteen or sixteen knots, Lucy was capable of scaling just about any surface the world cared to throw in her way. An unmoving wall of very old bricks whose mortar had been eaten away by time might as well have been a flight of stairs. She scrambled up easily, ignoring the dull twinges from her burned palm, and came to rest with her toes braced against the top of a window and one arm wrapped about the beam that projected out over the door.

The old rope that supported the shingle hung from a pair of iron loops on the underside of the beam. Lucy felt the tension on the rope, picked a single strand free to see how easily it broke, and worked out a reasonable idea of how much she'd have to cut before the rope could do the rest of the job on its own. Then she began severing a few strands at a time.

She'd gotten about two-thirds of the way through when the remaining strands began to whirl and split. Lucy scooted back toward the wall, then the beam itself gave an ominous groan. She flung herself off it and scrabbled for a handhold on the brick as the beam broke away from the wall completely and plunged to the road with a crash.

Exactly as she'd planned, the horse gave a shriek of panic and bolted. Lucy leapt down and fled into the passage just as the squeal of hinges sounded from the door of the chainwright's workshop.

She peeked around the corner of the building to see a tall, thin man with silver hair curling over his collar stalk away after the mare. "Get back here, you luckless beast," he snarled in a voice full of gravel. The horse slowed but didn't stop, so he had to keep on after her.

No time to waste. Lucy found the window with the cracked pane and gave it a sharp knock with the handle of her knife. The cracks stretched, then a huge chunk of greenish glass fell in and shattered. Lucy reached through, found the latch, and gave it a twist. The window swung outward with only a low whine of complaint.

She hitched herself up and through the casement and then she was inside. Despite a few candles burning here and there, the space was mostly dark except for where daylight from the open door bisected the room. There was just enough illumination for Lucy to be certain this was a smithy. Glancing around, she spotted a gleam of metal: a collection of sharp-edged steel on a workbench beside the cold furnace. Surely finding the Albatross wouldn't be as simple as taking it from a pile of blades lying in plain view?

Still, it was a place to start. She dashed across to the bench and began carefully moving things aside in search of the peculiar blade that Trigemine had described.

Then she stopped and her heart tripled its already furious beating. Trigemine's description of Christopher Swifte had been very specific: tall, muscular, and *black*. The man who'd gone after the horse had been tall enough, but although his skin had been darkened by forge work, he had been white: Jonas Forgeron himself, most likely. In any case, the man who'd left the shop had not been Swifte, which meant . . .

A deep voice spoke from the back of the room, flavored equally with warning and amusement. "Can I help you find something, girl?"

Lucy dropped one of the knives she had picked up. It sank blade-first with a thick, soft *thunk* into the floor as she turned to face the voice. A man rose from a table directly beside the window through which she had come. He had been sitting right there the whole time, close enough that his heavy boots crunched on the glass she had broken as he took a step toward her. A second man at the table folded his arms and leaned back, as if to enjoy the spectacle of whatever happened next.

Rutting land. Rutting, shifting, prigging, quiffing, buggle-arsed land.

Christopher Swifte was exactly as Trigemine had described: tall, dark-skinned, and powerful, with a deep scar across his neck. Lucy had seen enough scars to know this one must've been the result of a terrible wound. By what miracle had he survived it?

"You've come from Trigemine," he guessed. Lucy stiffened as he reached into his jacket and pulled a knife that could only be the Albatross from a sheath under his arm. "You've come, I imagine, for this."

It was a dreadful thing, dreadful and beautiful at once, the way a ship on fire was dreadful and beautiful. And Lucy sensed that, just as a burning ship contained within it the far deadlier threat of the massively explosive powder magazine, somehow this knife might also be hiding a greater menace between its sharp edges.

She glanced toward the open front door, but just then the big toast-colored mare ambled up and stood swishing its tail in the cobbled street, presumably while the gray-haired man tied her to her post. There was no escape in that direction, Swifte now stood between her and the broken window, and there remained the third man, the one who still sat at the table, to factor in. These were bad odds.

With no way out and facing the hook-bladed knife in Swifte's powerful hand, Lucy could do nothing but tell the truth. "Yes, sir."

Swifte shook his head in disgust. "Just like his kind, sending a child to steal what can't be bought. Put that down, girl," he added, eyes on Lucy's right hand, which, out of some instinct her left one lacked, had held on to the other blade she'd picked up from the workbench. "There is no fighting with me."

It was neither boast nor threat; it was merely a statement of truth, and Lucy believed him. She lowered the knife onto the workbench with the rest.

At that moment the gray-haired man stepped through the doorway, grumbling. He glanced from Swifte to Lucy and back. "Oh, don't tell me," he groaned.

"Trigemine," the man at the table said. "Sending children now, Jonas." She'd heard his voice before. Lucy looked closely at him for the first time: it was Jianming Cerrajero, the sailor who'd put her on the trail of the *Driven Star*. *I must thank him,* she thought irrationally. *If I survive this, and he doesn't have a hand in trying to kill me.*

Forgeron, meanwhile, went to a stove by the furnace. "That's low, even for Morvengarde," he replied, picking up a kettle and pouring hot water into a mug. Tea? Was he making himself *tea?*

"I am standing here, you know," Lucy said under her breath. Then, louder, "What now?"

"What now?" Swifte asked, surprised. "Now you leave, of course. You don't imagine I'm going to hurt a child simply because it was fool enough to find itself mixed up with Trigemine, do you?"

"Well, I rather did, I suppose," Lucy said in some confusion. "So . . . I may leave?"

"You had better," Swifte retorted.

"Maybe through the door this time," Cerrajero suggested, eyeing the shattered glass under the window. Forgeron snickered into his mug.

Lucy was so relieved to find that she wasn't about to be flayed with that frightful hooked knife that she nearly fled. But halfway to the door, she stopped. She faced Christopher Swifte with a quiver in her heart. "I cannot leave without it," she said in a voice so small, it was barely audible.

Swifte raised an eyebrow. "I beg your pardon?"

Lucy swallowed and forced herself to speak more loudly. "I cannot go without the Albatross."

"I told Trigemine I wouldn't sell it to him," Swifte said. "It follows, then, that I won't give it to him for free. You ought to figure that if I wasn't going to let you steal the thing, I won't give it to you either." He slid the knife back into its sheath.

Forgeron regarded Lucy curiously. "How did you come to attempt the sutler's thievery for him?"

The sutler had to be Trigemine. "He and his compatriot have taken my brother for a hostage."

Cerrajero unfolded his arms. "I recognize you. You're the girl who was after a boat. That was your brother, then? The boy whose mother's name I apparently insulted?" He glanced at Forgeron. "His mother shares a name with the daughter of a legendary emperor. An ordinary name, usually. A name you'd give to a little boy. The emperor's daughter's name, however, was supposed to mean 'Shines in the Night.'"

The other two men spoke in unison. "Ah."

"That makes sense of things, I suppose." Forgeron sat down on a stool beside the door and propped his elbows on his knees. "That's quite a predicament to find yourself in. Why you?"

"What do you mean, why me?" Lucy snapped. Swifte had called her a child, and he had called her *it*. Now this question, which was somehow insulting despite also being perfectly reasonable.

"To come after the Albatross. Why not a professional thief?" he asked. "Why not someone stronger, or someone with some sort of skill?"

"I have skills," Lucy said indignantly. "I grew up on a letter-of-marque!" Not that she seemed to be able to make any of those skills work on land.

"Which is what?"

"A privateer, Jonas," Cerrajero said. "Perhaps she is something like a thief, after all."

"I am not *anything* like a thief! Privateers are not pirates! A letter-of-marque is *licensed* to fight for the crown."

"Then why you?" Forgeron persisted.

"Why does it matter?" Swifte asked.

Forgeron waved a hand impatiently. "Who is your brother?"

"Just a boy. He's seven."

"Then who's the other man? Trigemine's compatriot?"

"I don't know! Just a—a peddler. A fireworks peddler."

He stroked his chin. "Called Blister, perhaps?"

Lucy blinked. "How did you know?"

The old man's eyes took on a predatory sort of glint. "We are not unacquainted, Ignis Blister and myself."

"And who are *you*, precisely, sir?" It seemed reasonable to ask, since the chainwright hadn't condescended to introduce himself so far.

He smiled frostily. "Jonas Forgeron is my name, for now. I am Grandmaster of the Worshipful Company of Whitesmiths, sixth in precedence among the Chapmen's Guilds, and a Founding Member of the Confraternity of Yankee Peddlers. Not that I think it's quite the thing to ask unless one plans to return the introduction."

Lucy tried to make her own voice cold too. "Melusine Bluecrowne, daughter of the owner and master of the *Left-Handed Fate*, a private ship of war under letters of marque and reprisal from His Britannic Majesty, George the Third. I am called Lucy."

Jonas Forgeron rose and extended his hand gravely, and Lucy shook it. She wasn't certain what a whitesmith was, but his hand had a familiar feel. It was very like the *Fate*'s blacksmith's hands: hard-skinned, strong, and covered in ancient burns.

"Now that we are acquainted," Forgeron said, joining Swifte and Cerrajero to sit at the table by the window, "who was it exactly who took your brother, Lucy Bluecrowne? Trigemine or Blister?"

"Blister. My brother is fascinated by incendiaries, and Blister was teaching him a particular formula."

"Ah."

"What does this mean, Jonas?" Swifte asked.

"It means the boy is not simply a hostage. It seems strange to think of a conflagrationeer of Blister's caliber being involved in the taking of a boy with similar talents if . . . well, if that weren't actually the *point*."

Lucy shook her head. "But they were working together. Surely Trigemine wouldn't offer to give Liao back in exchange for a knife if Liao is so very important to Blister, would he?"

Forgeron touched his finger to the side of his nose. "That is it, precisely. Or at least, having made the offer, he will certainly not follow through on it in any permanent way."

"Meaning—"

"Meaning," Swifte said, "Foulk Trigemine lied to you, Miss Bluecrowne. He sent you here because he decided there was some chance you might succeed, and since I had already told him I wouldn't sell the knife to him, it didn't matter at all if you failed." He leaned back in his chair. "And I think Mr. Forgeron is suggesting that even if you do succeed, Trigemine won't give your brother back."

Forgeron shrugged. "He might give him back to you, but not for long. If Morvengarde wants your brother, Trigemine will not— *cannot*—let him go."

It *had* sounded too good to be true, not that Lucy wanted to admit it. "And what is this Morvengarde?" she demanded, her face growing hot.

"He is the Great Merchant," Forgeron said, pronouncing the last two words as if they were a title. "And Trigemine, well . . ." He shrugged again. "There are many sorts of chapmen. Sellers of many things, and many kinds of selling folk; some are generally honest and some are not. Most keep at least a bit of integrity in a pocket somewhere and dust it off now and then when it suits them to use it. But sutlers are true parasites. The most ordinary of them are warbirds, following armies and profiting from the desperation of soldiers beaten low by violence and who must get shoes at any price or walk the next hundred miles barefoot. But roaming-world sutlers are as different from their everyday brothers as I am different from an everyday tinsmith. Men like Trigemine are perfectly capable of killing to make a profit. They are predators."

"I don't know what the roaming world is, sir, but—"

"But you know what a *predator* is, do you not? Trigemine is a predator, girl."

"What I *know* is that he has my brother and says he will give him back," Lucy argued. "*You* say he's lying, but he's the only chance I have!"

"He is no chance at all. He will take the knife, and if he gives your brother back to you, then he will simply take him again. To break a bargain is low, but if the alternative was to anger the Great Merchant Morvengarde, there are no depths I imagine he wouldn't sink to." The old man hesitated. "Furthermore, I know something you do not, a thing that tells me precisely how seriously these two are taking this abduction. And they are taking it very seriously indeed."

"What's that?"

Forgeron shook his head. "I cannot tell you. I would, if I had not been bound by promises I cannot break."

"But—"

The whitesmith held up a scarred hand. "There are rules about these things."

Rules? *Promises?* When a little boy's life was at stake? Apparently she wasn't the only one who thought it sounded absurd. "For what you lot can do when you want to, you're awfully rule-bound," Cerrajero observed.

"Enough." Christopher Swifte took the knife from its sheath again and set it on the table. All four looked at it. "It is merely a knife," Swifte said softly. "Until it is not."

Lucy followed the candlelight flitting over the metal feathers and scales. "What makes it . . . not?"

"Many things might do that. In this case Morvengarde has decided it is more than a knife simply through his wish for it." Swifte regarded the blade with a strange mixture of pride and wariness. "I made it because I wanted to make something beautiful and terrible."

"Why terrible?" Lucy asked.

"Because I am a weapons-maker, and all weapons are terrible." Swifte raised his eyes to Lucy. "You are a mariner. Can you guess why I shaped my favorite knife in the form of an albatross?"

Lucy considered. There was so much albatross lore. In some stories they were good fortune and in some they were dread creatures, worse luck than white cats and parsons. What sort of fortune they brought depended upon a great many factors. But Swifte wasn't a sailor as far as Lucy knew, and she had no idea how landsmen felt about the creatures.

She glanced at the knife. Knives could bring either sort of luck as well, depending—were they white-handled or black, chipped or whole—but, whether it roused favorable winds or terrible seas, a knife could always be made to cut a rope that wanted cutting.

Lucy looked at Swifte. "Because they might do good things or bad, depending upon how they are used, just as an albatross might be good luck or bad, depending upon how the wind blows?"

"You have it, precisely," Swifte said, sounding surprised and pleased. He touched the hooked blade. "I shaped it this way for no other reason than because it is how an albatross's beak is shaped. Yet the first man I showed it to . . . can you guess what he said?"

Lucy shook her head. "No, sir."

When he spoke again, Swifte's voice was flat, devoid of any inflection at all. "He commented that it would do nicely for tearing out a fellow's throat." He curved the index finger of his left hand, touched it to his neck, just to the side of his Adam's apple, and made a flicking motion.

Lucy discovered quite suddenly that there was a chance she might vomit.

"At the time," Swifte continued, "I did not mind that this was how he envisioned using my beautiful, terrible creation, because one cannot live on making weapons if one cares too much what the customers do with them. I also did not care because I had not made the Albatross intending to sell it. Mind you, I sold that man plenty of other things over the years."

"But now?"

"Now I find I care a bit. And so I refused to sell the knife to Trigemine, because I could see in his eyes that he saw it the same way that first man did."

"And who was that first man?" Cerrajero asked quietly.

Lucy suspected everyone present already knew the answer. "Was it this Morvengarde fellow?"

"It was indeed," Swifte replied. "And now you come to me, wanting to take my knife to these men at a time when, for whatever reason, I have begun to care."

He contemplated the Albatross for another moment, then eyed Lucy thoughtfully. "I will make you an offer, Miss Bluecrowne. If you really believe that Jonas and I are wrong, ask me just once more and I will give you the Albatross so that you may take it to Trigemine and try to strike your bargain."

After all this, after everything he and the old whitesmith had said, Swifte was offering her the knife freely? She reached a tentative hand toward it. "You'll *give* the Albatross to me?" She couldn't quite bring herself to touch the thing. Her body warred with itself; her heart ached to leap while her stomach was already sinking with the suspicion that these men were right, and that Trigemine's bargain was a lie.

Swifte eyed her fingers as they hovered inches from the feathered handle. "I will, if you ask it."

"She'll get herself killed with it," Forgeron warned.

"That may be," Swifte said, "but it will be her choice, and I will have given my creation to someone who believes it may do some good."

"You don't believe it will do any good at all." The words were bitter in her mouth. Her fingers tingled, twitched.

"But *you* do, which may be as much as I can hope for. Even if I think you are wrong."

"What if Trigemine takes it and this Morvengarde does something terrible with it?"

"There is no *if*. He *will* do something terrible with it. No one whose first response to an object is to remark upon how well it would tear out another's throat is likely to seek a gentle-hearted collector for it."

"But there is a *possibility* it will buy my brother back," Lucy insisted, trying to decide whether she really cared what became of the Albatross once she had Liao safe at home again. And trying to believe, despite everything Swifte and Forgeron had said, that Trigemine would keep his word.

"There is always a possibility." Forgeron set down his mug and folded his arms. "It's possible the ground at our feet will open up ten seconds from now and your brother will climb out of the breach unharmed. But the greater likelihood, when you deal with men who tend toward the wicked, is that nothing surprising will happen and they will behave exactly as you expect. They will behave like wicked men, and you'll be left wondering how you ever believed things would turn out otherwise."

Swifte looked at her intently. "And so?"

Her fingers itched to take the knife. Any chance to get Liao back, however small, was a chance she had to take. All she had to do was ask. Her hand hovered, curling toward the handle. *Ask,* she willed herself. *Say the words.*

Any hazard at all was worth risking. And yet . . .

She recalled something Trigemine had said. *If you can convince him to give it to you, by all means, do that. Simpler for all concerned, and not as impossible as it sounds.*

He had known. Trigemine had somehow *known* that Swifte

might make this offer. But how? And then abruptly she remembered something else he had told her, when she had complimented the stickpin in his cravat.

I use it to walk through time.

She had taken it for the sort of inane thing adults say to children for their own amusement, but that had been before he'd come into the parlor and vanished again so suddenly, as if he had simply blinked into nothingness.

He had known Swifte would make this offer, and he had known she would take it.

The weapons-maker watched her with compassion. It was his demeanor that made Lucy understand at last that he was right and that having the Albatross would not get Liao back.

Helplessness washed over her like a massive wave on a following sea. She pulled back her hand and dropped it to the table, and for a moment the aching surge actually made her sway. "Liao," she whispered, and her voice sounded like the voice of someone else—someone small and helpless. Someone useless. A child, which was what everyone from Swifte and Forgeron to Trigemine himself had been calling her all along.

People had called her a child before, but this was the first time in her life she could remember feeling like one. Not even after the splinter, when she'd been unable to walk on her own feet and Kendrick had carried her like an infant, had she felt so helpless.

Lucy touched the scar on her forehead with shaking fingers and the memory of that day came surging back, right down to the anger she had felt at being forced below. *I am not only a child,* she thought bitterly. *I have never been* only *a child.*

She met Swifte's sympathetic eyes. "Keep your knife," she said coldly. "I'll find another way."

"Well said." Cerrajero clapped his hands.

She flashed him a grateful smile. Then, without another look at the gleaming, beautiful, and terrible thing on the table, Lucy turned and strode fast and tall toward the door, tossing the words "I'm sorry I broke your window, Mr. Forgeron" over her shoulder as she went.

The old man shrugged. "Mayhap it'll give the room a nice cross-breeze."

As she stepped out into the lane, Christopher Swifte called from inside. "Wait."

Now that her eyes were adjusting to the brighter outdoors, Lucy couldn't see into the darkness of the workshop. She heard a dull whisper she thought might be the sound of Swifte re-sheathing his blade, the scrape of his chair moving back, then heavy footfalls and the hard, slithery skirr of metal on metal.

"Hang on a tick, Kit," Forgeron's voice said. "Find her something that'll take apart rope."

More metallic hisses, then more footsteps, then Swifte's massive shape filled the doorway. The hand he extended was burn-scarred, just like Forgeron's.

"Here." In his palm an object the shape of an eel gleamed: a curved, tapered steel spike with a slightly flattened tip. It was about the length of Lucy's hand, and its blond ash handle was inlaid with pale green wood in a delicate pattern of leaping fish. Swifte offered it to Lucy, handle foremost. "For you. A gift from the Ironmonger."

She took it carefully. The grip sat perfectly in her palm, comfortable in weight and flawlessly balanced. "It looks like a marlinespike."

"And a marlinespike it is," Swifte replied. "I have occasionally made things other than weapons."

"It's far too lovely for make-and-mend day," Lucy said uncertainly. A marlinespike was a necessary instrument aboard a ship, where they were used for knotting and splicing rope. Given the situation, she rather wished that instead of a seaman's tool, however beautiful, he'd given her a proper weapon.

"I would be very happy to know it was used for make-and-mend day. And I have no idea how much it will help you against Trigemine. No mere weapon will," he added, as if he'd heard her thoughts. Then he spread his hands. "But it's what I have to give, and I hope you will keep it."

"Wait." Cerrajero elbowed his way past Swifte, fumbling in his pockets. "I want to give a gift too." He withdrew his hand and held out a folding tool she'd seen him using on the lock when they'd met on John Agony Pier. "Give this to your brother. Tell him I take it back, what I said about his mother."

Lucy eyed the thing: a plain metal frame with a small assortment of little attachments nestled into it. Why could no one give her something she could fight with? "What is it?"

Cerrajero shrugged. "Just a thing I use on locks. Perfectly ordinary, I'm afraid, but ordinary has its uses as well."

Lucy tucked the gifts carefully into the ditty bag that still hung from her shoulder. "Thank you both."

Cerrajero nodded, and Swifte said, "Our pleasure. Get on your way now."

Christopher Swifte, Jonas Forgeron, and Jianming Cerrajero watched the girl rush down Holloware Row. "Do you imagine she has any chance?" Forgeron asked.

Swifte rubbed his scar thoughtfully. "I hope so."

Cerrajero laughed shortly. "It appears you've picked your side, Kit."

"Does appear that way, doesn't it?" Swifte sighed. "Guess I'd better find that Jumper."

"No need." They turned to see the bespectacled man called Simon Coffrett striding toward them from the other end of the street.

"Jumpers." Forgeron coughed far back in his throat and spat on the cobblestones.

Coffrett ignored him. He stopped before them and examined the shingle on the ground opposite the workshop door. "And so, Mr. Swifte?"

The Ironmonger regarded him for a moment without emotion. "It's yours, with one added condition."

"Name it."

"Get that girl's brother back from the sutler for her. You can do that?"

The Jumper tilted his head. "I can do a great number of things. But it isn't my place."

Forgeron laughed grimly. "Ah, the great mantra of the Jumpers. *It isn't my place.*"

"What did I say?" Cerrajero leaned against the wall and folded his arms. "Rule-bound, the lot of you. I wouldn't be a roamer for all the world."

"Rules can be broken," Swifte said, and each word landed like the strike of hammer upon anvil. "You want the Albatross, this is what it costs."

"If you're on her side," Coffrett said deliberately, "then do not set that condition." He looked at the small figure of the girl as she disappeared onto Fornax Street, and behind his spectacles, his eyes slid out of focus.

Anyone who had seen Trigemine doing chronometrical trigonometry would have recognized the expression on the Jumper's face: it was the countenance of someone working through infinitely complex calculations. Except, of course, Trigemine would have been working out figures on paper with the help of a battery of computing tools, and Simon Coffrett appeared to be doing nothing more than watching a young girl turn a corner.

"No," he said at last with the beginnings of a smile, "I do not think you want me to intervene. She has what she needs."

Forgeron stared. "Do you have *any idea* what she's up against?

Do you have any idea what it would take to best Blister and Trigemine when they're already girded up for taking on a demigod? Or does she have some power we didn't spot?"

The Jumper waved a hand. "Not all powers are magic. I suspect as the daughter of a privateer, the girl herself would be the first to tell you that in a battle, tactics and strategy are as much of the fight as force. Watching for unexpected opportunities. Seeing that the ones firing the guns have what they need. And sometimes I imagine in the end the greatest victories come down to sheer, thickheaded courage."

"What's the smile for?" Cerrajero asked.

"She reminds me of someone else. That's all." Coffrett turned to Swifte. "What is your decision, Mr. Swifte?"

The Ironmonger hesitated. "She can get him back, then? They'll be all right?"

"You want a binary answer, yes or no, and that answer doesn't exist," Coffrett said. "I can tell you only what I have already said: that she has what she needs. If that isn't enough for you, then I can do no more. What is your decision?"

They regarded each other for a long moment, then Christopher Swifte reached into his coat and unbuckled the shoulder strap he'd worn there for years. He held the Albatross out, still nestled safely in leather.

"I accept," he said simply.

Simon Coffrett took the sheath carefully. "Thank you. I'll be waiting for you in Arcane when you're ready."

Swifte exhaled, and when he inhaled again it seemed that a decade at least had fallen from his face and body. "I think I have a few more years of walking in me."

"Walk as long as you wish. I'll be waiting whenever you choose to come home."

"Home," Swifte said, pronouncing it as if it were a word in a language he did not speak.

TWELVE

XIAOMING

IT was nearly five o'clock in the evening when Lucy tied up the *Driven Star* beside the pier at the bottom of the cliff. Her father and the *Fate* were too far away to help rescue Liao, but perhaps she and Kendrick and Garvett had a chance.

She took the stairs as fast as she could, then forced her aching legs to carry her across the shadow-streaked lawn to the house. The door opened as she reached the porch and Lady Xiaoming stalked down the stairs to meet her. Her dark eyes swept over Lucy and the lawn behind her. "Where is Liao?"

Lucy opened her mouth and choked on something bitter. Words stuck to her tongue. "I—I lost him, Jìmǔ," she managed at last. Xiaoming blinked. "He was taken," Lucy added, rushing to speak before her stepmother did. "By the peddler, the one we met the day we bought my boat."

"The one who was coming to teach Liao his particular blue,"

Xiaoming supplied impatiently. "I remember." She glanced at the ruins of Liao's workshop. "But Kendrick and Garvett could only say Liao was nowhere to be found after the explosion."

Lucy shook her head. "He was taken," she insisted, and the rest of the story tumbled from her in half-coherent mouthfuls.

"This peddler took Liao?" Xiaoming asked slowly when she had finished. "Or was it someone else?"

"It was the peddler himself." Lucy braced herself for the fury that had to be coming. *You lost my son.* She had never seen true anger from Xiaoming before today, but surely it would be a storm the likes of which Lucy could never have imagined.

Xiaoming stood, stony-faced, for a moment. "Kendrick and Garvett have gone for Richard and the *Fate*." Lucy's heart plunged. Without them, she had no chance.

"Come inside and tell me everything you remember." Xiaoming's voice had all the knife-edge of a Baltic wind, but the storm did not come. Lucy's mind raced as she followed her stepmother up the stairs and inside, where she sat meekly in one of the chairs beside the hearth.

There was a pot of tea steaming on the table beside it, along with a full cup that Xiaoming must have been just about to drink. Instead, she put it into Lucy's shaking hand. "Take a sip, and then tell me what you recall."

The tea was thin and strong and Lucy wished it were coffee, but it cut through the sour flavor at the back of her mouth. When she'd finished half the cup, she began talking, beginning with when they had met the peddlers in the Quayside Harbors. Xiaoming paced the length of the parlor, mostly listening in silence but interrupting now and then to ask a question. At last, Lucy could think of nothing more to tell. She fell quiet, waiting for her just punishment.

Still it didn't come. Instead, Xiaoming did something odd: She took one of the carved pins from her hair and bent to put it among the glowing coals that were all that remained of an earlier blaze in the grate. Then she turned to Lucy. "I need to see his wares. Whatever's left of them. Show me." Her face remained stony, but as Lucy stood, her stepmother reached out and scratched her shoulder gently: once, twice. Lucy couldn't decide whether it made her feel better or worse.

Together they hurried back out and across the lawn to the remains of the workshop. "Let it be a lesson, Lucy," Xiaoming said. "It does not do to ignore the little voices that whisper when something is not right. These creatures should never have been able to touch my son," she said bitterly. "But I did not listen, and now . . ." She picked her way through the debris, kneeling here to lift a scrap of paper, there to rub her fingers across the surface of a charred stone.

"You . . . you knew there was something wrong?"

"Yes, and if so many things had not been new and unsettled here, I should have realized how very wrong indeed that something was. But we ignore our instincts far too easily."

Lucy nodded fervently. Looking back, she could see half a dozen times it ought to have occurred to her to wonder about the peddlers. Liao himself must have had an idea, or he wouldn't have stopped her from telling Xiaoming about the improbable daylight fireworks he had made.

She wrapped her arms around herself as her stepmother worked her way through the rubble, torn between relief that she hadn't been shouted at and impatience to be doing something, *anything*. "Jìmǔ, how does this help us?" she asked.

Her stepmother raised a finger coated in shimmering blue powder and touched it lightly to her tongue. Then her eyes narrowed and a thin smile stretched her lips. "It tells me what we are dealing with." She brushed the powder from her hand and straightened. "And it tells me why he has taken Liao. Come. We cannot wait for your father."

Back in the house, Xiaoming swept up the staircase, leaving Lucy in the parlor with a single barked command: "Wait." Lucy stared helplessly into the cup of lukewarm tea on the table. She almost wished Xiaoming had unleashed hell on her. She should have. Lucy deserved it.

Light footfalls sounded on the stairs, and her stepmother returned with a lacquered box in her hands. She strode past Lucy, drew a stool to the hearth, and sat with the box on her knees. From inside it she took a brownish object. It was roughly triangular in shape, like a partly closed fan, and covered with a variety of darker markings, some stained black or brown and some in shades of red. These embellishments, which reminded Lucy immediately of scrimshaw, made her realize that she was looking at a piece of bone.

With her other hand Xiaoming reached into the fireplace for the hairpin she had tucked among the coals. She held up the pointed tip and blew on it, and though it didn't seem possible—not given the rapidly cooling coals it had been nestled among—the pin's end reddened and began to glow: first scarlet, then violet, then blue. Lucy stared. How was it heating up that fast? And how was that heat neither incinerating the pin nor traveling up it to singe her stepmother's fingers?

If it caused her any discomfort at all, Xiaoming ignored it, right along with Lucy's open-mouthed confusion. She held the bone up by the narrow fan end. On one face, it was highly polished and inscribed with columns of symbols and the faded traces of what looked like a delicate and complex crisscrossery of fractures. On the other, scores of small, blackened hollows had been bored in on either side of a raised ridge that ran from top to bottom. With her eyes on the polished face of the bone, Xiaoming pressed the smoldering end of the pin into one of the hollows on the reverse. After a moment, with a percussive *pak pak pak* sound, a series of new, razor-thin cracks erupted on the front. Xiaoming stared at these for a moment, then inserted the pin into a different hollow, this one on the opposite side of the bony ridge on the back, and another set of cracks materialized. She looked at the fractures for a second or two, then she exhaled: a slight, piqued sound.

Lucy watched in fascination as her stepmother repeated the ritual, using another pair of hollows to cause the bone to crack again, *pak pak pak pak, pak pak pak pak*. This time, whatever information they conveyed made her face darken abruptly, and she uttered a phrase in Mandarin that Lucy had no trouble identifying as a curse.

Without waiting for the pin to cool, Xiaoming threaded it absently back into her coiffure. Lucy winced at the sudden smell of singed hair, but Xiaoming didn't appear to notice. She set the bone aside and reached into the lacquered box on her lap once again. This time she produced a dull gold vial, which she uncorked and lifted to her mouth.

"What's that?" Lucy asked, not sure if she meant the contents of the vial or everything she'd just witnessed.

"Medicine." Xiaoming drank, then resealed the vessel. She closed her eyes and held very still for a moment.

Lucy studied her intently. "Medicine for what?"

"Many things."

"And what . . ." Lucy glanced at the fan-shaped bone on the hearth. "What about that bone?"

"It is an oracle bone. The shoulder of a deer. It is tremendously old. I asked it two questions." Xiaoming's voice took on a formal tone. "And the lady divined that to attempt this battle alone would not be auspicious, and reading the cracks the daughter of Shun said, 'to attempt this battle alone would bring disaster.' Thus is the first question answered."

Wide-eyed, Lucy glanced from her stepmother to the scapula bone. "All that, just from the cracks? Who's the lady? Who's the daughter of Shun? What was the second question?"

"Both of those titles belong to me," Xiaoming said, returning the vial to the box. And as for the second question—" She regarded

Lucy with an odd expression. "Will you help me bring Liao back?"

"Yes, yes, of course!" As if she would have agreed to stay behind. "Was that the second question? Is it . . . is it auspicious if I help?"

"There is . . . the possibility of less harm," Xiaoming said cautiously. "But it will hurt."

Lucy opened her mouth to say that it didn't matter, that she didn't care, that she would do anything, *anything* to have her brother back. But something about the combination of Xiaoming's words and her strange demeanor made Lucy pause.

Her stepmother nodded. "Good. You should know more before you answer." She reached into the box again, and this time she took out a sheet of yellow paper and a red pencil. "This creature who took Liao—if it is the same one who compounded what I found outside—he is not merely a peddler, not merely a pyrotechnician. He is an *artificier*. He is drawing upon truly ancient knowledge from a great art called *wàidān,* which takes many lifetimes to accumulate. The peddler has at least some awareness of *wàidān,* or of something very like it."

Liao had said something about *wàidān* too, though Lucy wouldn't have remembered the word if Xiaoming hadn't said it herself. *What I do . . . it's not* wàidān *at all,* he had said. *It's just chemistry.* "And how do you know about it?" she asked warily. "This *wàidān?*"

"My family has seen a great many masters of methods in the arts of *wàidān.* I am one."

"But if it takes that long to learn . . ."

Xiaoming gave her a half-smile. "I have told you I am older than I seem." She leaned in to the hearth and took a piece of half-burned wood from the ashes. As she held it between her fingers, the charred end began to change color, and from under the mottled ash rose a hint of pink. It warmed to a cherry color before Lucy's eyes: fire, coming to life.

"That's—that's—" *Magic* is what she wanted to say. She thought back to Liao the day before, talking about how Blister had said he was different. *I wonder if he somehow knows about my mother.*

"It is spectacle," Xiaoming said dismissively, tossing the glowing bit back into the hearth. Immediately a slick of fire burst from it like a shoot bursting from a seed. "Spectacle is easy, and meaningless. But if I told you what *wàidān* really is, you would neither understand nor believe me. So for the moment, think of it as . . . let me find a word . . . *sorcery*, perhaps. Liao does not have this sorcery. He is not yet a *fāngshì*, a master of methods—but he will be. That is why this peddler has taken him."

So he *was* different, then. "But if Liao could be magical but isn't, why bother with him at all? Why not come straight for you? If you already have . . . *it*, whatever it is?"

Xiaoming shook her head. "Imagine a cutter, a schooner, and a frigate."

Small, medium, large. "All right."

"Liao is the cutter, and the peddler is the schooner. There is almost no risk in the schooner's engaging the smaller boat. But he should think twice about engaging the frigate, which will have double the guns and hands as he himself does, and against which his chances are so very much smaller. He *could* take the frigate, but it is much more likely that he will lose both his ship and his life."

"And you're the frigate in this tale?"

"No, Lucy." Xiaoming's eyes sharpened. "I am a ship of the line."

Lucy's jaw dropped. Xiaoming was comparing herself to a vessel with twice or three times the force of a frigate. "A *ship of the line?*"

"Yes. But I will still need help. To keep to the metaphor, even a great ship of war sometimes needs her boats." She placed the yellow paper on the lid and drew a column of red symbols on it. "I will need *your* help, Lucy, and it will hurt. Are you willing to suffer some pain to rescue our Liao?"

Lucy swallowed and fidgeted with the ditty bag. "What do you mean, it will hurt?"

Xiaoming laid down her pencil. "It will feel like dying."

Like *dying?* "Why can't you do it?" The words were out before she'd thought them through, and immediately she was ashamed. *Behaving like a child,* she thought, disgusted.

Her stepmother, however, didn't seem bothered by the question. "Because I will have another part to play, and I cannot do both. And before you ask, even if I was willing to change places with you, you are not a *fāngshì* and you cannot undertake the other task."

"But I won't die?"

"No, you won't die. Not from the pain I fear I must ask you to suffer, anyhow. But it will be dangerous from beginning to end, until you have gotten away with Liao and both of you are safe. Any of us could die in the process."

"All right." Pain *like* dying was not the same as dying. She could handle pain. And really, facing the possibility of death—well, that was daily life at sea.

Xiaoming eyed her solemnly. "It seems like an everyday expectation to you, doesn't it? Confronting the worst and soldiering through it, whatever might happen. We say *chīkǔ*—'to eat bitterness.' You sailors are very good at this." But instead of being pleased, she seemed sad.

"What's wrong?" Lucy asked.

Her stepmother gave a small sigh as she returned the red pencil to the box and set it on the floor beside her stool. "The saddest thing a mother or father must learn is that one cannot protect one's children from hurt." Without warning, she reached into the newly kindled fire, and before Lucy could so much as cry out, her stepmother's hand was buried deep in the flames. "I would gladly keep all the pain in the world for myself," Xiaoming murmured, "but that is not possible."

An unfamiliar and disagreeable scent began to thread its way through the aroma of burning wood. Xiaoming winced and withdrew her hand, and in her blackened fingers was the same cherry-red coal that had started the blaze. As she returned to the table beside Lucy's chair, she touched the coal to the bottom edge of the yellow paper, which began to darken and curl.

The scorched edge rose, consuming the slip and its red symbols bit by bit, and small black flakes began to drift downward into the teacup that sat, forgotten, on the table. Lucy kept her eyes on the ashes floating on the cooling yellow-green surface, not wanting to look too closely at Xiaoming's burned fingers. Neither of them spoke, and in a matter of moments the paper was nothing more than a soft pile of slowly sinking ash.

Xiaoming picked up the teapot and poured more tea, then reached into the cup with her charred index finger to stir the mixture. Then she lifted it with both hands and held it out. "Drink."

Lucy took it uncertainly. "What . . . what is this?"

"An elixir. The paper is called a *shényìn*. A talisman, you might say." Her eyes were impatient. "Drink, Lucy. Liao is waiting somewhere, and we are taking too long."

Lucy lifted the cup to her lips and sipped. The tea tasted like scorched things now, and the cinders tingled as they passed her tongue, as if they were still red-hot.

"Drink it all." Xiaoming's eyes glittered. "With this elixir, you can walk through fire."

Wide-eyed, Lucy kept on until she had swallowed every drop. Then she wiped up the slurry of ashes at the bottom with one finger and ate those, too.

"Good girl," Xiaoming said. "I must have one final question answered, and then we will go." Lucy flinched again as her stepmother thrust her hand once more into the flames.

Xiaoming held it in the fire longer this time, and as Lucy looked on, horrified, the pain hardened her stepmother's face into a mask. At last Xiaoming pulled her blackened hand from the fire and used it to lift the oracle bone again by its narrow neck. *Pak pak pak pak pakpakpakpakpak!* A web-work of glowing cracks snaked instantly across the polished surface like rivers drawn willy-nilly on a map, like a Gordian knot of impossibly tangled cordage, like the web of an insane spider.

As the popping sounds of the spreading fissures intensified, Xiaoming turned the bone over. On the reverse, five of the circular hollows flushed with blue-white heat. Lucy watched breathlessly as Xiaoming held up her empty hand and spread her fingers wide, fitting one to each incandescent cavity. A heartbeat later, with one final shattering *pop,* the shoulder bone disintegrated into slivers, but her stepmother barely seemed to notice as they cascaded to the floor. Xiaoming stared at her hand as if memorizing the exact manner in which she was holding it, from the space between each finger to the angle of her wrist.

Then, finally, with a whisper of satisfaction on her face, she turned to Lucy. "Now, take me to this peddler."

✦

Lucy laid the *Driven Star* alongside the listing pier where Blister's little rowboat bobbed on the sunset-red river. She made the cutter fast, hopped out, and held it steady for Xiaoming.

"There," she said, pointing to the shape of a house in the trees. Her stepmother followed the gesture and started up the path without a moment's hesitation. "Jìmǔ, wait!" Lucy protested, grabbing for Xiaoming's sleeve. "They'll see us coming, if they haven't already. There must be another way in." If this were a cutting-out expedition, how would her father go about it? "If we go around the hill and come up to the back of the house, we might find a servants' entrance, perhaps."

Xiaoming shook her head, eyes cold. "We are equal to these foxes, and equals enter by the front door."

"But they'll know! We'll have no surprise on our side!"

"We have strength on our side, and the weather gauge, too. Have I used the term correctly?"

A ship that had the weather gauge had the wind on its side, which meant that ship could bring the fight to its opponent. Certainly they were bringing the fight, but in this situation, Lucy had no idea whether that gave them any advantage at all. And she still didn't know what to think about Xiaoming's claim that she carried so much more force than the peddlers. "This is a bad idea," she whispered.

"What does your father like to say about Lord Nelson? Something about not wasting time with maneuvers, and to go straight at the enemy?"

"He likes to tell that story, but he never *fights* by it! Papa *always* uses maneuvers!"

But in the end all Lucy could do was scurry along in her stepmother's wake as she strode up the path to the house, took hold of the bell pull, and gave it one short, sharp tug. The sound of a chime echoed within, and a moment later, the door opened.

Trigemine stood on the threshold. His frigid blue eyes regarded Xiaoming for a moment before they lighted upon Lucy. "Well, well," he said in a tone more suited for greeting a long-lost friend than addressing an enemy. "If it isn't the young privateer." Now his eyes flicked back to her stepmother. "And a very beautiful someone I have never met." He swept his tall round hat from his head and lowered his chin, but his eyes remained glacial, and they did not leave Xiaoming. "Come right on in."

"Very kind." Like Trigemine's, Xiaoming's gaze was unwavering. Lucy thought of a shot fired across the bow of an enemy ship, the shot meant to warn the foe to strike its colors quickly, before things got ugly.

The sutler stood to one side, just enough for them to pass. Xiaoming swept past him. Lucy followed, wondering how her stepmother was keeping her poise.

Ignis Blister's voice called from somewhere deeper in the house. "Who is it, Foulk?" There was a musical noise, a quick twanging scale. *Plink-a-plink-a-plink-a-plink.*

Trigemine didn't answer right away. Instead, he turned his eyes on Lucy and arched an eyebrow inquiringly. *Where is my knife?* his frosty expression demanded.

Lucy didn't know how to answer a question with her eyes, especially when what she really wanted to say was *You're a liar and you never meant to give Liao back and I know it,* so she settled for staring him down.

The peddler narrowed his eyes. "Did he not offer it to you?" He sounded troubled.

"He did," Lucy replied. "And I said no."

The tall peddler's eyes lit up with a fury so cold, it was all Lucy could do not to curl up in a ball on the floor and whimper.

Somehow she managed to hold herself upright, but every muscle fought it.

Trigemine gave the smallest of shrugs. "You're on your own," he said quietly, and in a bizarrely kind tone. Then he kicked the door shut and put one of his big hands on the back of Lucy's neck. She froze. A warning grip, neither hard nor unfriendly—not yet. But she could feel the strength, the threat in it. One false move and this man could break her neck or crush the life out of her, and he wouldn't even need to use his other hand.

"I do not like to be disappointed," he whispered gently. And then, raising his voice. "We have a pair of callers, Blister. I suspect they're here to talk to you about the boy."

Xiaoming turned and regarded him. "It is not polite to put your hands on others uninvited."

He smiled, and the gulf between his tone of voice and his expression deepened. "But we're old friends, Lucy and I. In fact, I sort of thought she might be bringing me a present." He gave her neck a gentle squeeze. "But she didn't, so now I'm not sure we're friends at all. Which is regrettable, really. If you make an enemy of Blister, you need all the friends you can find."

"Perhaps it is for the best," Xiaoming said coolly. "As it happens, Blister has made an enemy of me, so it rather seems *he* needs all the friends *he* can find. You had best not desert him now." She held out one slender hand to Lucy. "Come along. It sounds as though we will find him in the garden."

Now, *that* was a warning shot if ever there was one. Lucy

swallowed and stepped forward, out of Trigemine's grasp. He didn't precisely let go, but he allowed her to step away. Lucy felt his fingernails scrape her skin as she did, and she knew she would find welts there later. If she survived that long.

Xiaoming's eyes narrowed. "If you touch my daughter again, I will end you."

There was no change on Trigemine's face. "The garden's that way. Through the parlor and straight on back," he replied. His voice was so cordial, yet his eyes promised violence. "I'm right behind you."

Xiaoming put a hand on Lucy's shoulder and drew her forward into the parlor. "We are not foxes, Lucy," she said quietly. "Leave the creature in your shadow, where he belongs."

There was a soft noise like a snort from Trigemine. Xiaoming scratched her shoulder gently—once, twice—and Lucy stood up just a bit straighter. She forced herself not to look back and walked with her stepmother through an open pair of glass-paned doors and into a courtyard.

The garden had seen better days. It was overgrown, full of tangled bushes and vines that choked the half-hidden shapes of statues, fountains, benches, the closed door of a gate hung with trailing creepers. In the deepening twilight, those dark forms seemed to crouch, menacing and monstrous, as if they might pounce at any false step. Sconces peeked from the ivy on the walls here and there, and in each one a yellow candle burned.

Ignis Blister, smiling blissfully and plucking the strings of a small, round-bodied guitar, sat on one of the benches. Beside him stood a tall, mottled blue taper—tallow, from the smell of it—burning in a bone-colored candlestick covered with carvings. In the center of the garden was a pillar of fire the azure of deep water under a clear sky, and in the center of the pillar stood a small human shape. He was burning alive.

Lucy screamed. *"Liao!"* She darted forward a step, stumbled, halted. There was nowhere to go. Between Lucy and her brother the wall of fire burned ten feet high. But now she could see that inside his fiery prison, Liao was not, in fact, being immolated. He didn't appear to be frightened, either; he was *angry*. He said something and pointed, incensed, at the peddler, but his very words seemed to sizzle into nothingness as they attempted to pass through the flames.

Xiaoming took no more than a cursory glance at the pillar that imprisoned her child before she turned to Blister. "I am Xiaoming, daughter of Yu Shun, styled Chonghua, who reigned for fifty years as the last of the Three Sovereigns and Five Emperors. That is my son."

"Ignis Blister," the peddler shot back. "Founding Member of the Confraternity of Yankee Peddlers and Grandmaster of the Worshipful Company of Firesmiths and Candescents, fourth in precedence among the Chapmen's Guilds. Son of a gun and a quickmatch." The instrument in his hands gave a few lazy *pling*s under his fingers. "And it looks to me like the boy's mine now, *princess*."

"Step back, please, Lucy," Xiaoming said in a voice like a blade.

The air in the garden felt charged, as if every bough and leaf were crackling with electricity. Xiaoming and Blister regarded each other, she disdainfully and he indifferently, for a long moment.

And then, without warning, Blister burst into flame. Only for a heartbeat, though—in fact, it happened so briefly that Lucy almost thought she had imagined it. One moment he was fine, the next he was burning, engulfed head to toe in fire the color of melted gold. Then the fire was gone and the carelessness had fallen away from Blister's face. Now he was *enraged.*

"Fool woman," he snarled. He raised a hand and for a moment Lucy saw the round shape of a linen bag in his palm. It ignited, and Blister flung it at Xiaoming. She didn't bother to duck or even to flinch, and the crackling ball of light hit her squarely in the chest. Like Blister, she burst into flame, and small, licking tendrils of cobalt fire rushed over her.

But something else happened too. Lucy blinked and stared from behind the statue where she had taken cover. The figure outlined in flames was not Xiaoming. Or at least, it was not Xiaoming as Lucy knew her.

It was as if the familiar shape of her stepmother had been a shadow, and the sky-colored fire now illuminated what that shadow had been concealing. This new form was still recognizably a woman, but instead of the robe and loose trousers she had been wearing before, this woman was cloaked in white-gold feathers. Beneath Blister's flames the feathered woman glowed from within, like a smoldering coal.

She lifted her arms, and they were no arms at all but wings like a crane's, tipped with long black feathers. The wings beat once in Blister's direction, and the blue fire swept away from her and back toward the peddler like dandelion seeds on a puff of wind. Except these dandelion seeds were licks of flame, and when they hit Ignis Blister, he screamed. To Lucy there looked to be as much astonishment as pain on his contorted face.

Lucy tore her eyes from Blister to glance at her stepmother, who was now an unchanged Xiaoming once more, and then past her to the doorway where Trigemine stood looking just as discombobulated as she felt. His eyes met Lucy's, and he began stalking toward her, keeping well away from what was happening at the center of the courtyard.

The thought *I shan't be another hostage for you* pierced Lucy's shock, and she backed away, fumbling in her ditty bag for Christopher Swifte's marlinespike. Blister was still burning and howling while Xiaoming appeared completely untouched, so as long as Lucy kept herself out of the mix, perhaps this would be over quickly and there would be no need for her to do whatever it was that Xiaoming had warned would feel like dying.

She yanked the marlinespike from her bag and held it up between her and Trigemine. "New toy?" he said. "How about you put that down before you hurt yourself?"

"Keep back!" It was like brandishing an oversized needle as if it were a sword, which perhaps might possibly have been helpful to someone who knew how to use a rapier. Lucy could wave a cutlass as a last resort, but that was all. She glanced over her shoulder, wondering how long she would need to hold him off.

Just at that moment, Xiaoming stepped up to the pillar and raised one hand with her fingers spread. It was the same awkward position she'd held them in to match her fingertips to the glowing hollows in the oracle bone in the moment before it had shattered. Now she touched her fingertips to the surface of the fire. Instantly, a web-work of gleaming cinnamon-colored lines radiated outward from her hand, just as the web-work of cracks had streaked across the surface of the shoulder bone—only here the fissures branched and forked and combined to fashion the shape of an arched doorway against the blue of Liao's prison. Then, at the same moment, the still-burning Blister leapt onto Xiaoming's back with a length of bright silver cord stretched between his hands, and Trigemine, brandishing his knife, leapt at Lucy.

Lucy stabbed at him with the marlinespike. Trigemine dropped his own knife and fell back. His coat sleeve flapped, and a smear of red bloomed through the cloth. "What the hell is that?" he roared, clutching his arm just below the elbow.

I cut him? "A gift from the Ironmonger," Lucy said in a shaking voice. *I cut him!*

"*That* came from the Ironmonger?" Trigemine demanded. "He *did* give you a weapon, the bastard! Just not the one I wanted." The sutler swore. "I *knew* there was something odd about those reckonings." For a moment he lifted his hand away from the wound and took a step toward Lucy. Then he swore again as a fresh gout of blood spattered the ground at his feet, and he clamped his palm back down on his arm. "This isn't finished, girl. Blister, are we done here?"

With the marlinespike still held out toward Trigemine, Lucy whirled to find the other peddler stepping away from a huge white crane with black-tipped wings and a crimson face that lay on the ground, bound with the silver wire he'd been holding when he'd leapt on Xiaoming's back. Blister's clothes hung from him in scorched tatters, and wherever his skin showed through the fabric, it was cracked and charred red and black. His expression, however, was triumphant.

"No!" Lucy gasped.

"Yep. Forgeron's rope did the trick, though *damn* but whatever she threw at me *hurt*." Blister licked his burned lips. "I . . . I have been aflame before, but I have never actually *burned*. Fascinating." He looked down at his scorched hands with his brows knitted in wonder and consternation. "I didn't know that I could." He eyed the reddish portal still flickering against the blue flame as he picked something up and examined it with interest: one of Xiaoming's carved hairpins, which must have been knocked loose in the struggle. Liao flung himself against the door again and again, but either Blister had stopped Xiaoming short of finishing or it simply did not work. Her brother was still just as trapped as before.

"Now, put down the knife, girl," Trigemine said patiently, gently, his eyes glittering with vitriol. "There's nothing left for you to do."

The crane stared up at Lucy with one round, unblinking eye. *I would gladly keep all the pain in the world for myself, but that is not possible.*

"Yes, there is," Lucy whispered.

With this elixir, you can walk through fire.

She took a step toward the door in the burning pillar.

"Take care," Blister warned. He tossed the hairpin on the bench beside the candlestick and held out his blackened and smoldering arms. "This is not painless cald-fire whose burn can be ignored. This is lyke-fire, and it will burn through to your very soul before it kills you."

It will feel like dying. Lucy thought of ships catching fire, and how they burned, and how they exploded, and she shuddered. Then she thought of Xiaoming, plunging her hand not once but twice into a blaze. She thought of Liao, trapped behind that wall of flame. She stepped up to it. She squared her shoulders and took a deep breath, and then she stepped through. And she screamed.

THIRTEEN

LYKE-FIRE

T could only have taken a moment, walking through the curtain of flame, but it felt like an eternity. It felt like all the pain Lucy could imagine. It felt like all the pain of hell. It felt like death and more, and it felt like that forever. Then she was lying in a heap and Liao's arms were around her and he was crying and saying her name over and over and still she screamed. At last she opened her eyes and discovered to her shock that she was not burning, and by slow, aching degrees, the pain subsided.

"Lucy, Lucy, Lucy," Liao said. Lucy hugged him weakly, then gently disengaged his arms and stood. Looking through the fire was like looking through water, and the twilit world outside seemed to have been bled of color.

Trigemine and Blister peered through at her, shadow-toned, like sculptures cut from different shades of gray-hued marble. Trigemine was saying something, but just as Liao's words had sounded like the sizzle of oil in a hot pan when she'd been outside, now that she was within, the sutler's voice was nothing but noise like the creaking of icebergs. Still, the gist of what he'd said was plain enough: *How the hell did she do that?* Blister shook his head, stunned.

Liao still sobbed, but now he couldn't seem to decide whether he was sobbing about Lucy's obvious pain, or about what had happened to him, or about what had happened to his mother. And what *had* happened to his mother? There was the Xiaoming-bird, still trussed in gleaming wire, still staring at Lucy with those black-marble eyes. It gave the slightest tilt of its head. *Go.*

Go. But how? Xiaoming's talisman had allowed Lucy to walk through Blister's fire, but Liao had no such protection as far as Lucy knew. And even if she could carry him safely through it, Blister and Trigemine were waiting on the other side. She and Liao would still be trapped.

Meanwhile, the peddlers were conferring. Finally Blister stomped to the carved beige candlestick and plucked the tallow candle from its socket. He licked his thumb and forefinger and pinched the burning wick between them. But when he let go, the flame popped up again, dancing as briskly as ever.

Visibly surprised, Blister looked from the candle to the pillar of fire. He spat on his fingers and tried again to put the taper out, and still the flame kept on burning. He reached into his pocket, pulled out a pair of wick-trimming scissors, and snipped the burning bit right off. He stared at the pillar, plainly expecting something to happen, but nothing did. Nothing, that is, except that a flame reappeared immediately on the fresh bit of the taper's wick. Furious, Blister snarled something at Trigemine, then jammed the candle back into the candlestick and sprinted into the house.

"Blister can't put the fire out. That candle must control it somehow, but it isn't working." Lucy glanced down at her still-crying brother. "Liao, you've got to buck up now. Your mama said it was up to me to get you out if anything went wrong."

Liao could not tear his eyes from the bird. Whatever he was thinking, he didn't seem to have words to express it. She reached down and pulled him to his feet. Something small and golden glittered from the collar of his jacket.

"Liao, what is that?" But even as she asked, she knew what it was and where he had got it. She had seen something similar in Trigemine's cravat: a slender engraved stickpin.

I use it to walk through time.

Lucy raised her head sharply. From the gray world beyond the flames, Trigemine met her eyes, and instantly she recalled what he'd said back in the parlor: *Away, and out of your reach forever. And this is what it will look like.*

He reached into his pocket as Lucy tore the pin from Liao's collar and flung it to the ground. It vanished, and so did the sutler.

Blister returned from the house to find his compatriot gone. He stopped in his tracks, then leapt nearly out of his shoes as Trigemine reappeared without warning next to him. If he'd been enraged before, Lucy didn't have a word for the sutler's anger now. He balled his hands at his sides and let out a howl of fury that Lucy could see, but not hear.

"They cannot put out the fire, and they cannot take you away without the pin." Lucy allowed herself the smallest sigh of relief. "We're safe so long as we are in here." That was something.

What was it she was meant to do? Xiaoming had foreseen the pain, but the rescue wasn't over yet. The talisman had changed Lucy somehow so that she could walk through flame. What else could she do?

"Liao," she said slowly, "Jìmǔ gave me a talisman. That's how I came through. Can you tell me what else it's for?"

Liao blinked, eyes still glued to the bird. "A talisman?"

"Pay attention!" Lucy snapped. He looked up guiltily. "A yellow paper. She wrote something upon it in red and burned it, then I drank it in a cup of tea."

"A *shényìn*?"

"Yes. What does it do?"

"There are many of them," Liao said. "They do all sorts of different things." He wiped his eyes, which were still welling up, and took a few shuddery breaths that were probably meant to help calm him down, though they didn't seem to work. "I'm sorry. That's not very helpful."

"That's all right." Lucy turned in a circle as Blister paced outside. *The talisman made me different. But different how?*

She thought back to when she had drunk the talisman, to the prickling effervescence on her tongue. Feeling foolish, she spoke aloud. "Fire?"

A ripple of movement swept across the dancing inner surface of the pillar, and Lucy felt as though a breeze had wafted over her. The flames billowed, almost like a sail in the wind.

Liao's eyes popped. "Are you *speaking to the fire?*"

"I don't know," Lucy whispered.

"Try it again!"

"Fire?" Lucy said experimentally. The flames billowed again. Hope welled in her chest as she saw a solution—if, in fact, this blazing pillar was actually, miraculously, listening.

She took a step toward the closed garden gate, and then another. One more step brought her to the limit of the space inside the pillar. The wall of flame was inches from her nose, and her heart began to thud with fear, with the memory of agony.

"Fire," she whispered, "fire, walk with me."

And then she stepped forward, and the wall of flame moved.

"It did what you said!" Liao gasped. "Do it again!"

Lucy took another step, and again the pillar moved with her. It was impossible—and yet it was happening. The fear rushed from her heart. If she could command the fire, perhaps she could also douse it when the time came. She put an arm around Liao. "Stay by me. We're going for that candle."

Holding him close, Lucy sprinted for the bench where the candlestick that held the undying candle sat beside the hairpin and Blister's round guitar. Both men lurched into motion as well, but Lucy reached the bench first.

She stretched a hand through the fire. The searing this time was just as unbearable as before, and, blind with pain, Lucy snatched the candlestick as well as Xiaoming's hairpin. Blister, seconds too late, picked up his instrument by its neck and slammed it onto the bench in a fury.

Inside the pillar, Lucy put her arm around Liao again. "Let's go now."

He pulled away. "We can't, not yet!"

"Liao —"

He clutched Xiaoming's hair ornament to his chest. "Not without my mother, Lucy!"

As if it had heard him, the bird raised its red and white head and let out a warning squawk. Its eyes radiated admonition. *Stop wasting time.* Lucy tightened her grip on her brother. "I don't know how to free her, and we've got to get clear of this place."

"Try!" Liao begged, tugging away again. "Please, Lucy!"

One try, then. She turned toward the heaving shape of the crane under its binding. Jonas Forgeron's voice came back to her: *Find her something that'll take apart rope.* She glanced around for the marlinespike she'd dropped when she'd first come through the pillar. An ideal weapon it was not, but for this work, a marlinespike was perfect. Blister's silver cable plainly could not be trusted to behave like ordinary, everyday cordage, but maybe, just *maybe,* Christopher Swifte's spike would be up to the challenge.

She found it just within the perimeter of the pillar, then, with her brother at her side, she returned to where the crane lay. She handed Liao the candle, braced herself, and reached through the wall once more.

Oh. It was terrible, unbelievable. Outside the wall, Trigemine was shouting *Stop her,* the words visible on his lips even though Lucy could hear only that iceberg creaking, but there was no need for anyone to stop her—she was completely immobilized by the pain. At her side Liao was crying again, and she realized she was screaming. Her fingers curled into the marlinespike's handle so hard that she thought they might break.

It was the spike that brought her through it. She could feel the inlaid wood in her bandaged palm, could feel the muscles that held it. She couldn't stop screaming, but somehow she managed to move her hand to one of the silver lines. Then she realized she needed her other hand to pull the cord away from the bird's body.

Beside her Liao was begging her to breathe: *Breathe, Lucy, breathe.* She stopped screaming long enough to obey, then plunged her left hand through the wall, willing it to do what she needed it to do before the pain destroyed her resolve. On the other side of the fire, two hands that did not seem to belong to her pulled the cord away from the bird's wing and slid the flattened tip of the marline-spike into the woven metal, separating out a single filament as fine as a spider's web. With one flicking motion, she broke the line.

It gave way with a sharp, surprisingly loud metallic *ploing.* As fast as she could, Lucy teased out another filament. The crane gave a mighty heave as Lucy snapped that thread, and that was all it took. The strands of metal began rending one after another, and with a final flail from the crane to help it along, the cord split into two. The ends whipped apart so hard and fast that anyone who'd been in the way would have lost a finger, or worse.

Both peddlers dove for the bird, but she flung her wings wide and burst free in a flash of black and white and scarlet. Her wings beat at the peddlers in a single powerful *whoosh,* and as Lucy fell backward, dragging her own arms out of the inferno, she saw Blister and Trigemine sprawl back as well, clutching their faces and covering their eyes as if they had stared into the sun. Then the crane turned and shot Lucy a glare that was at once reproachful and sympathetic. *Go.* It spread its wings and rose into the air.

Go. The lyke-fire wavered. Lucy shoved the marlinespike into her ditty bag and put her free arm around Liao again, this time to keep from crumpling, and her too-small brother held her up as well as he could. Both peddlers were cradling their heads, unable to open their eyes.

"Walk with me, fire," she whispered, and the fire carried Lucy and Liao from the garden.

Trigemine lay with his face to the earth, howling. Even with his eyes closed the world was blinding, excruciating. But the girl and her brother were out there somewhere, outside this world of light and agony behind his eyelids, and time was flying.

He let out one last tortured shriek and rolled to his back with the heels of his palms pressed into his eye sockets. "Blister?"

The peddler spoke from somewhere off to his left in a tone that was equal parts anger and agony and awe. "Damn me, but that was the greatest blast I've ever seen." From the scratch in his voice, it seemed Blister had done some screaming of his own, not that

Trigemine had noticed. "I have *got* to figure out how to replicate that luminosity."

"Never mind the blast." Slowly Trigemine took his hands away from his eyes, then blinked until the details of the world began to separate themselves from the remnants of the light-blindness. Little by little, the brightness became nightfall once more. Blister's lyke-fire prison was no longer there, but a path of scorched earth showed where it had been, and where it had gone.

Trigemine pounded a fist on the ground, shoved himself to his feet, and checked his vest pocket. Mercifully, the kairos mechanism was undamaged. From his trouser pocket he took his notebook and flipped it open, one-handed, to the page upon which he had copied the previous night's workings.

"How long, how long?" he muttered, squinting to make out his writing in the deepening darkness. Then he flipped the notebook closed, shoved it back in his pocket, and hauled Blister upright. "Get up. We might just have time. Move!"

The peddler rubbed his eyes. "What do you mean, we might *just* have time?"

"The window. The moment of kairos. It isn't endless and everlasting. Can you do anything more to stop her? We have time for perhaps one more try."

"Can I . . ." Blister laughed miserably. Then he shook his head as if to clear it. "But you can just take us back, can't you? Back to before this all went wrong? Damn them!" Blister flung an arm at the bench. "My banjo! And my candle! They took my candle, the mongrels! *But look at my banjo!*"

"No, we can't just go back. We have to take them *now*. I explained this, Blister." Trigemine stalked to the open garden gate and considered the track twisting away down the hill. "You can't walk back and forth endlessly. There are consequences each time."

"Worse consequences than if we fail?" Blister asked grimly.

Trigemine shuddered. "Let's not find out. Can you stop the boy's mother?"

Blister rolled his head on his neck, cracking it. "There is a thing I can try. A kind of fire called belluine." His expression twisted, and it looked so odd on him that Trigemine had a moment's difficulty identifying it—Ye gods, was that actually *fear?* It was gone before he could be certain.

"Why the hesitation?" Trigemine asked, unsettled. "Any special reason you didn't try this belluine thing before?"

"Yes," Blister snapped. "Two reasons. In the first place, I've never actually used it, so I'm not certain exactly what it will do. I don't know if it will work at all on a being as powerful as she is, but it's the only thing left that I know of that might. *If* it works, we lose any chance at *taking* the lady. And if it doesn't work—maybe even if it does—you'll be on your own once I cast it. Belluine . . . " That expression flashed over his mug again, and this time Trigemine saw it for what it was. The mad conflagrationeer was terrified.

Blister's eyes met his. "I didn't know I could burn, you see," he said quietly. "And I will burn for this." He glanced over at the bench where his banjo lay shattered. "Mongrels," he added, disgusted.

Out of the garden, down the wooded hill. The pillar of fire slid through the trees, cauterizing branches and incinerating bracken so completely they didn't even appear to burn, just fell away instantly to ash that swirled like a leaden snowfall against the bleached world outside.

At last, the pillar came to the tilting pier. Inside the column, Lucy and Liao glanced at each other. "Now what?" Liao asked.

Lucy looked back the way they'd come. The peddlers were nowhere in sight. She raised blue the taper. "Fire, go out now," she said, and just as she had seen Blister do, she licked her thumb and forefinger and pinched the wick.

There was a stabbing pain in her fingertips, and another in her bandaged palm Lucy lowered her hand. The wick smoked, but the flame did not come back to life. Around them the pillar flared once, blazing skyward, and died. The sounds of the world rushed in, and for a moment, despite the darkening night, the colors of the autumn woods on the river were blinding.

"Well done, Lucy."

Liao gave a squeal of delight and ran onto the pier. Lady Xiaoming stood beside the cutter, looking tired in the moonlight but otherwise just exactly as she had when she'd stepped off this same boat earlier in the evening. She took her missing hairpin from Liao and tucked it back into place.

Lucy followed, exhausted, in her brother's wake. She had so many questions, but all she could manage was "Are we safe?"

Xiaoming's eyes flicked from Lucy to her dazed son and then up the slope toward the house. There was a trail of singed ground, frizzled creepers, and smoldering trees, but nothing more. The woods were quiet.

"You are safe," Xiaoming said. But her face was drawn and there was something in her bearing that was at odds with her words.

For his part, more than anything else, Liao seemed oddly sad. "What is it?" Lucy asked, kneeling beside him. Immediately she regretted it. Her legs felt like two giant puddings. *I shall never be able to stand again,* she thought wretchedly.

"I know he was a very bad man," Liao said, speaking haltingly in the way he did when he was both working through a thought and figuring how best to express it in English. "But he said something that made me . . ." He paused. "That made me feel something good. He said, 'You will set the world on fire.'"

"I'm sure he did." Xiaoming's voice was hard. She knelt as well and put a hand to Liao's cheek, and when she spoke again, her voice was gentle and so full of love that Lucy's chest ached.

"I wish something like that for you, Liao," his mother said. "*Light* the world. There is a difference." Liao shook his head, confused, and Xiaoming spoke briefly to him in Chinese, probably repeating the same words to be certain he understood. "You, too," she said, returning to English and scratching Lucy's shoulder with her other hand. "Light the world."

Then she stiffened. "I love you both," she said softly, quickly, and perhaps because she spoke in English this time, Lucy heard the goodbye in her words and understood with a sudden wash of dread why her stepmother had replied to her earlier question in the way she had.

You are safe.

Xiaoming stood and turned in a single, fluid movement, shoving both Lucy and Liao behind her as a ball of liquid flame the color of fresh blood appeared on the hill. It tore across the sky, making a noise like a scream as it sliced through the air—no, like *two* screams, in nightmarish, not-quite-harmony with each other—and there was something about its flight that made Lucy think of a huge and galloping beast with muscles flowing under its pelt, a feral thing whose coat was ablaze and whose legs carried it through the ether faster than the eye could follow. It left a second, smaller, man-shaped conflagration behind it at the top of the slope, and Lucy could just make out Blister's voice, raised in mindless pain, as half of the ghastly shrieking chorus.

The blood-red comet struck Xiaoming full in the chest and its terrible fire swarmed over her body. For a moment they saw her crane form, a dark silhouette against the licking crimson light. Then the shape came apart like a firework exploding in the sky, and Xiaoming was gone in a rain of vermilion sparks.

FOURTEEN

TAKE, SINK, BURN

"*MAMA!*" Liao screamed.

Lucy grabbed hold of him, numb with shock. "Jìmŭ?" *This can't be. This* can't *be.*

Liao shook loose and reached up with frantic fingers, as if somehow by catching the fading flashes of light he could put his mother back together again. But these were not shreds of a person—Lucy had seen plenty of people blown to bits, and this was nothing like that. The sparks raining down on them now reminded her precisely of the ones that fell like snow when one of Liao's better rockets exploded overhead. Or—the thought hit her with the force of a punch—the swirling ashes of the incinerated branches that had accompanied their passage down the hill only moments before.

Disbelief and horror and heartsickness battered at her, but there was no time to indulge those emotions. Lucy tore her eyes from the sight of her brother howling and chasing glowing ash. The fireball had come from up the hill, and there, of course, were Trigemine and Blister. The smaller peddler was no longer afire, but he clutched at his partner as if he could barely stand.

"Into the boat!" She grabbed Liao by the collar of his shirt. "Liao, we have no time. Go!"

Wailing, he allowed himself to be hauled to the *Driven Star*. But with every step Lucy took, her heart sank further. The night lay thick and still around them. There was no wind on the river any longer, and the cutter couldn't carry them to safety without a breeze.

Another ball of fire flew past, missing the *Driven Star* by a hair's breadth. Amid a little avalanche of loose rocks and brown leaves, the two peddlers were scrambling down the incline: Trigemine rapidly, Blister more slowly, as if he could barely stand.

Lucy dropped Liao into the bottom of the boat, steadied the craft with quick, instinctive movements, and cast off. The sail hung limp and motionless. "Out sweeps," she shouted, yanking one of the ancient oars from its hooks. Her brother looked around, probably, she realized belatedly, for a broom. "Take an oar, Liao!" She jabbed her own at the pier, but the blade was so rotten that it gave out spongily as she tried to get the boat moving.

Liao paused in the act of trying to pull another oar from its place and gave a delighted shout. "See there, Lucy!"

Moonlight glinted upon a sleek schooner that had just appeared at the bend in the river. She was coming down the channel at the center of the Skidwrack as fast as art could make her go, but even fast ships with crack crews needed wind, and only the smallest ripple of white bow wave showed at her sides. The *Left-Handed Fate,* coming to the rescue. But slowly, far too slowly.

There was a stab of crimson, a puff of black smoke, and a barking explosion, and Lucy heard the *whine-splash* of an iron ball skipping across the water toward them. A warning shot meant for Lucy and Liao's pursuers, but the *Fate* was too far out of range to fire more than that.

Trigemine, however, didn't seem to understand how useless the schooner was at this distance. He shook Blister off and burst into a run, charging at the pier and sprinting across its uneven surface as Lucy finally got the *Driven Star* moving away.

Liao waved his oar defensively, but it was an ineffective weapon in the boy's small hands. Trigemine grabbed hold of the blade and yanked, nearly dragging Liao over the low gunwale and into the water. Lucy caught the tail of his shirt, saving him from going overboard but hauling the boat back toward the pier at the same time. "Let go, Liao!" she shouted.

He obeyed, and Trigemine flew backward with the oar in his hands. Lucy leapt onto the gunwale, put one foot against the pier, and kicked off as hard as she could. The boat drifted away again as Trigemine rushed at them once more.

This time he jumped. One heavy boot landed on the gunwale and slid right off, and Trigemine dropped into the water. The cutter lurched sideways as he scrabbled for a grip and found one.

Liao gestured frantically. "Lucy!"

"I see him." But it was hard to climb into a boat from the water, especially without help from someone inside. Pulling a person *out* of a boat was easier. "Stay back or he'll drag you over. I'll think of something." She dashed to the tiller at the stern of the listing boat. She needed to bring the *Driven Star* about and head for the *Fate*.

"Not him, Lucy!" Liao's voice had taken on a note of hysteria. "Blister!"

She turned just in time to see the other peddler, who had limped onto the pier at last, raise one charred arm. In his palm was something sparking, something ablaze. His face was twisted; for the first time, it seemed to cause Blister pain to hold one of his conflagrations.

"Stop!" he ordered. "Stop, or I'll turn that boat into a floating inferno." His voice was brittle, and the hand that held the fire shook.

Lucy halted in her tracks, but her eyes kept moving. There were provisions in the cutter, some from her cleaning and some from the cruise she and Liao had taken the day before. She made a speedy inventory: tar, oakum, a small barrel with Chinese characters written in chalk by a child's hand—one of Liao's homemade powder blends.

Trigemine stopped trying to pull himself aboard, and when he spoke next, his words were gentle. "Give me a rope. No, never mind that. Toss one to Blister."

Lucy shuddered. His voice was so *soothing*. Reassuring, even. As if the only reason Lucy and Liao might hesitate to follow his instructions was fear that they wouldn't be able to cast the line far enough. *You can do it,* his tone said.

His eyes, on the other hand . . . his eyes said, *I will tear you to pieces too small for baiting fishhooks.*

Liao clung to the opposite gunwale, just out of reach. "Why would we do that?" he asked, genuinely curious.

"Because otherwise I will kill you both," Trigemine answered kindly, fixing Liao with those frigid blue eyes. Lucy realized she'd seen blue like that before, in the deep southern latitudes where floating blocks of ice moved through white-capped water. Those were deadly too. "I'll kill you both," Trigemine repeated, still placid, "and the hell with how much trouble it gets me in. If I'm going to lose you either way, I'll damn well slaughter you and have that satisfaction at least."

A flash crossed the bow of the cutter, so hot and bright that Lucy felt the heat upon her skin like a sunburn: a warning shot from Blister, accompanied by a howl of agony. He crumpled to his hands and knees on the pier, and faint trails of smoke drifted up wherever he touched the old boards.

She squinted over her shoulder toward the *Fate*. Still too distant, still moving too slowly. Her father was lowering out boats; she could see the lights of the *Fate*'s cutter and launch already. With crews to row them, they'd get here faster, but still not speedily enough to keep Blister and Trigemine from making good on their threats.

"The rope!" Trigemine ordered again. His gentle tone was beginning to fray a bit now.

We could jump overboard, Lucy thought in desperation. Most

sailors didn't swim, but Lucy could manage a serviceable stroke, and it was possible she could keep both herself and Liao afloat for a bit. Perhaps they might even make it to shore, although probably not the *opposite* shore.

If they jumped, however, that gave Trigemine and Blister the *Driven Star,* and so long as the peddlers could row, they would have no difficulty in catching two awkwardly swimming children. And even once the *Fate* came within range, her guns would be useless. Oh, she could keep firing warning shots, but it would be nearly impossible to aim confidently for the cutter with Lucy and Liao nearby and all but invisible in the water. If the *Fate* did manage to hit the *Driven Star* (here, despite the dire situation, Lucy felt a wrench of sadness at the thought of her little boat taking a shot amidships), it meant debris and flying splinters at best, and at worst, an explosion if Liao's powder caught fire.

All these realities flashed through her mind as the boat gave another lurch under Trigemine's weight. He had gotten one sodden leg over the gunwale. Lucy grabbed a boat hook and flicked the sutler's foot neatly into the water. He cursed as he fell back, and the boat gave another heave, shipping gallons of water over the side.

And then, with a pang that surprised her with how much it hurt, Lucy had the answer. It was so obvious she couldn't believe she hadn't seen it right away. Trigemine, however, being a landsman, would never anticipate it.

In war at sea, the idea when one met an unfriendly ship was to take, sink, or burn her. Taking the ship was best, but failing that, one could at least make certain the opponent couldn't use it any longer. The same logic sometimes applied if the enemy was likely to take your own vessel.

Perhaps Liao's powder catching fire was exactly what they wanted. She felt another flicker of sadness, but then she remembered the sacrifice Xiaoming had made, and after that the thing she had decided to do didn't feel like much of an expense at all. *This is what a ship is for,* she realized: first and foremost always, a thing for fighting with. No matter how much prettying was done to make it elegant. No matter how much it felt like home.

"Liao!" She gave Trigemine another jab with the boat hook and flung all her weight in his direction as he leaned out of the way. The gunwale he held dipped under water, plunging Trigemine under too. As he sputtered back to the surface, Lucy jerked her head at the powder barrel. "Liao, would we have time to get overboard?"

Her brother followed her gaze. His eyes lit up and he nodded, a perverse joy rippling across his face.

"Then do it," she made herself say, "and tell me when to jump." *I'm sorry, barky dear.* She fumbled in her ditty bag with one hand and found Cerrajero's folding tool. "Here." She tossed it to Liao, and mercifully he caught it unerringly with both hands.

Trigemine was still blinking water away, but he saw Liao head for the barrel. "Stop!" he snarled, abandoning the charm altogether and redoubling his efforts to pull himself up. Lucy swiped at him once more with the hook, and this time it snagged in his vest. Trigemine blanched and let go of the boat, reaching for his watch pocket with one hand and fighting to free the hook from his clothes with the other.

Lucy held tight to her end, trying to make things as hard for Trigemine as she could. Liao, meanwhile, worked a bit of fibrous oakum loose from the rest and twisted it into a fuse. He held this in his mouth as he pried the bung from the cask of powder with a blade extracted from Cerrajero's tool. He glanced up and grinned at Lucy with the makeshift fuse between his teeth.

Seconds later he had the fuse in the bunghole with the wooden stopper holding it in place. He lit one of the matches Blister had given him and touched it to the oakum. A rose-colored speck began to travel slowly but surely along its length.

Liao straightened as well as he could on the lurching boat and gave Trigemine a disdainful look. "You ought to start swimming," he suggested. "The other way."

Trigemine glanced at the cask, saw the short length of fuse. His angry gaze sharpened. But instead of letting go, he batted away the boat hook and gave one final, desperate heave that carried him over the gunwale as far as his stomach.

Liao shrugged and turned to Lucy. "Now we go," he said calmly, buttoning the tool into a pocket.

Lucy squeezed the gunwale in farewell. *Goodbye.* She grasped Liao's hand. "Take a deep breath. Jump out as far as you can. Keep calm and hold that breath until you can't any longer. Don't let go of my hand."

As Trigemine writhed aboard, Lucy and Liao scrambled onto

the gunwale. Holding hands, they leapt into the river. Trigemine's enraged howl pierced the night as the cold water closed over Lucy's head.

The moonlit sky gave her just enough light to make out the shape of Liao's face through the dark water: his eyes were huge black pits, but his pale cheeks were puffed full of air. Tiny constellations of silvery bubbles escaped slowly from his nose. *Good.* Holding tight to his hand, she kicked her legs, sending them—*please, God*—farther toward the middle of the Skidwrack.

The explosion came just as she was afraid to stay under any longer. First there was the flash: a sudden blast of green-tinged fire overhead. Then came a concussion of thunder that resonated unnaturally through the river.

Lucy stopped kicking and curled herself around Liao. The water surged and she couldn't tell if they were being driven down or sideways. Abruptly he began to fight against her, twitching and flailing with increasing desperation. *Out of air.* Lucy slid her arms under his and kicked as hard as she could against the press of water and toward the surface.

He was a small boy, but frightened and fighting, he was heavy. Lucy, however, was running on panic energies. It was the same surge of chemicals that had kept her from feeling the splinter that had nearly killed her on the deck of the *Left-Handed Fate,* and now it made her legs and lungs work harder than she would have believed possible.

She broke the surface and pulled Liao's head from the river

as she sucked her first breath deep. He sputtered and coughed up what seemed like a pint or two of water, then gulped air.

Debris cascaded like rain around them, but these bits were falling rather than hurtling at the speed of bullets. They would leave bruises, not killing wounds. A short distance away on the tossing surface of the river, the flaming wreckage of the *Driven Star* was going down slowly as it burned. Its mast and yard, hung with smoldering scraps, poked up at wrong angles like the charred and broken bones of a giant's arm.

Emerald explosion, golden wrack. *Light the world,* Lucy thought, choking on a mixed mouthful of water and crazed laughter that tasted of deep relief and sadness. *Hail and farewell,* Driven Star.

Somewhere on the other side of the wreckage Trigemine was shouting at Blister, who now lay in a shuddering, unresponsive heap on the pier. Lucy ignored them and started hauling herself and Liao downriver. Perhaps one or both of the peddlers could swim. She didn't stop to look. The flaming hull on the water between them would hold up any pursuit for a bit, anyhow. She fixed her eyes on the schooner and the two smaller boats sprinting ever nearer, and concentrated on keeping Liao's head above water.

A moment later another shot from the schooner whizzed over their heads. She heard it skip across the surface of the river behind her. She didn't turn, just kept on flinging her free arm out and kicking her legs, towing her bedraggled and delighted brother along.

"Lucy," he was saying in between mouthfuls of water. "Lucy, did you see? My powder went up *green!*" A short wave hit him in the face and he sputtered for a moment. "Just wait until I try that wonderful blue."

He would soon recall what had happened before that emerald explosion. Through her exhaustion Lucy managed to wish that he would think about blues and greens for just a bit longer before he remembered.

After the shot came skipping past mere feet from him, Trigemine would've thought twice before plunging after the girl and her brother, even if he had known how to swim. It was already all he could do just to flail his way back to the pier where Blister had collapsed.

He heaved himself out of the water and coughed until his lungs felt functional, then lay back on the uneven boards until he could breathe without agony. Blister was yelling something, or perhaps it was just more screaming, but there was a blunt, heavy pounding in the sutler's ears that rendered the other man's noise into a dull mush of sound, easy to ignore.

Trigemine reached into the watch pocket Lucy Bluecrowne had somehow not managed to mangle with that infernal boat hook and took the kairos mechanism from it, though he already knew what the device would say. "We're finished," he said, more to himself than to Blister, and stared at the little pin that marked the brief space in time during which he had calculated their mission was possible.

His ears went on thudding painfully from the blast, so he could hear neither his own words nor the renewed barrage of shrieking they provoked from Blister. But he could feel his own racing heartbeat, amplified somehow by the thick sensation in his head that was the result of being so close to the explosion. And he could feel his own rising fear. He could taste it.

Morvengarde was not going to take the news of their failures well. There would be penalties, and they would be severe. Morvengarde, after all, had to answer to Jack Hellcoal.

It was going to be very unpleasant for everyone involved.

A voice came from his side, replying as if Trigemine had spoken out loud—which he had not. "Truer words, my friend. Truer words."

It was a familiar voice. Trigemine felt simultaneously as if someone had dumped ice melt down his spine and like he badly needed to vomit. He turned his head and looked at the woman who squatted at his shoulder, forearms propped on the knees of her impeccably tailored trousers and gloved hands clasped lightly between. "Miss Deacon."

"Trigemine," said the newcomer, looking down at him from under a velvet riding hat with a huge red peony tucked into the band. She was pale and fair-haired, and she turned flinty gray eyes on the peddler sprawled a few feet away. "Mr. Blister." She gave a short, terrifying giggle, presumably at the rhyme. *Please God, never let me hear her laugh again,* Trigemine thought, not remotely for the first time. Probably not for the last time, either. If God was listening, apparently he figured Trigemine deserved what he got.

Blister rolled achingly to his side and stared up at her. "Deacon?" he repeated in a thready, cracked voice. "*Seleucia* Deacon? Morvengarde's—"

She turned her reptilian eyes on the peddler. Not a muscle below her neck appeared to move. "Yes, Mr. Blister. So sorry I haven't been able to introduce myself properly before now. I wish we were meeting under different circumstances."

She applied no particular emphasis to those last two words; she might have been expressing a wish to have met in better weather. But the menace was there, radiating off Morvengarde's junior partner like heat off a rock in summer, so it wasn't hard to intuit the unspoken end of the sentence: *Under different circumstances, where perhaps you pair of fools didn't fail quite so spectacularly.*

Trigemine hauled himself up to sitting. "How long have you been here?"

"Long enough," Seleucia Deacon said. From the pocket of her waistcoat she took a round, gold object covered with engraving and whorls of black enamel and swung it gently before his nose by the fob. It wasn't quite a twin to Trigemine's kairos mechanism; from what he'd seen of it before, her device looked more like a conventional chronometer. It did a similar job, though. "I was expecting to be handed a knife and a conflagrationeer," Deacon said mildly. "Instead I arrive just in time to see you lose a battle with a woman you never should have tangled with, and neither Albatross nor salamander in evidence. Other than the salamander you brought to the dance," she amended, giving a casual nod of her chin in Blister's direction.

"Lose a battle?" Blister repeated, his indignance coming out a bit like a whimper. *"Lose a battle?"* With still-smoking fingers he shook his charred clothes at the merchant. "It nearly *killed* me, but I blasted her out of existence!"

Deacon's eyes widened. "Did you *really?* Oh, many pardons. My mistake." Trigemine winced as she laughed again. "Don't be ridiculous, Blister. You knocked her out of her body, that's all, and when she comes back, you had better already be dead." She turned to Trigemine. "Tell me about the Albatross."

Trigemine cleared his throat. "The Ironmonger has quit his profession. He chose to pass the Albatross to a Jumper from someplace out in Louisiana Territory, rather than sell it to Morvengarde."

You couldn't unsettle Seleucia Deacon. The slight twitch of her eyebrows was about as much confusion as Trigemine had ever seen her betray. At least he didn't have to defend his reckonings. Deacon's grasp of chronometrical trigonometry surpassed his by an order of magnitude, and she would have done the same calculations he had.

"Well." She clapped her hands, and the gloves gave the sound a gunshot quality. "Then I guess you know where you're bound. Someplace out in Louisiana Territory."

Trigemine stared at her. "The window of kairos closed. Hard. I did the reckonings. So did you."

Her reptile eyes stabbed through him. "Things get more difficult when you don't have kairos on your side, certainly. Things can get damned near impossible. But you are Foulk Trigemine, and my partner and I have faith in your capabilities. Fortunately." She rose, and took two steps so that she towered over Blister. "Now you. Explain."

Blister got to his feet and stood, still faintly smoking, before her. They were exactly the same height, but somehow she still managed to make the peddler look small, an effect that was heightened by the fact that even standing was too much for him just then. He swayed and grabbed for one of the pier's listing pilings in an effort to keep himself upright. "I am a Founding Member of the Confraternity of Yankee Peddlers," Blister said, brushing his smoldering gray hair into place with his free hand. "I am Grandmaster of the Worshipful Company of Firesmiths and Candescents—"

"Fourth in precedence, et cetera," Deacon finished, looking disturbingly like she wanted to yawn.

"I have known your partner," Blister persisted doggedly, "since the days when he called himself Drogam Nerve and drove a pony trap around this country just like the rest of us. I believe I have the right to speak directly to him." Then he slid to his knees on the pier, breathing hard.

Deacon looked down at the hunched, aching man. "And *I* believe," she said coolly, "that if he were here, Mr. Morvengarde would tell you that since he no longer goes by that name, invoking it does not confer any special *rights* upon you or anyone who knew him when he did. And may I remind you that in addition to being a partner in Mr. Morvengarde's enterprises, I am Grandmaster of *my* company, which is *second* in precedence among the Chapmen's Guilds, so you will kindly know your place, sir."

Before Blister could gin up a reply, another voice spoke into the silence. "This is good theater and whatnot, but I'd like to know where my firestarter is."

A man in a felt hat and a long leather coat sat on the bank to the side of the pier, leaning lazily against a large carpetbag. His face was youthful, with the exception of his eyes, which were lined and bitter and glittered the pale green of Nagspeake glass in the glow of a punched tin lantern that sat at his elbow.

Oh, no. Trigemine got up, trying and failing to look like he'd been going to do it anyway. Blister raised his head, but that was as much as he could manage. Seleucia Deacon closed her eyes briefly, then turned, putting herself, somewhat to Trigemine's surprise, between them and the man on the bank. "Jack," she said.

"Lu," he replied, smiling.

Trigemine and Blister exchanged a glance. *How is he even here?* Trigemine wondered. There would certainly have been a Jack Hellcoal in this era, but the contract with Morvengarde had been made with the Jack from Trigemine's own time, half a century later. So which Jack was this? If it was Jack-of-1810, how did he know to be here now? And if it was the Jack-of-years-to-come, how had he arrived here from then?

Apparently unbothered by paradoxes, Jack Hellcoal folded his arms and nodded to the schooner on the Skidwrack. "My conflagrationeer's on that boat?"

"So it would seem," Deacon said tightly.

"Who is it?" Jack inquired.

Seleucia Deacon turned her head ever so slightly, referring the question back to Trigemine and Blister.

The peddler answered. "A boy named Liao Bluecrowne."

Jack made a thoughtful face. "Must've been a force to be reckoned with to have slipped the two of you."

"He doesn't know his capabilities yet," Blister said cautiously. "But yes. And of course, he had help."

"Oh, he had *help*." Jack snickered, and the lantern rattled as he got to his feet.

"The boy's mother is an immortal," Deacon put in. "*'Help'* is perhaps understating the matter. And"—she frowned at Trigemine—"there was a girl." Of course. It might have been Lady Xiaoming and Liao himself who had done the heavy lifting involved in the rescue, but Seleucia Deacon had seen the endgame, and, un-like Blister, she had not underestimated Lucy Bluecrowne.

"His sister," Trigemine said quietly. "A privateer."

Jack stepped up onto the pier and looked past them all at the vessel that was busy recovering the Bluecrowne children out on the river. "Well, judging by Mr. Blister's condition, I'm guessing the four of us ain't taking a ship today. So how about you start suggesting ways to make this right, Lu."

She nodded once. "I'll work out the next opportunity."

He scratched his head under his hat. "That's not quite what I meant." He opened the door of the lantern, and as Trigemine, Blister, and Deacon watched, he put his entire hand inside and wrapped it around the object that was emitting the light. Through the punched tin sides, Trigemine could see Jack's hand begin to glow.

Then he took his hand from the lantern and shook it once, wincing. He reached for Deacon's nose with an incandescent finger. To her credit, she didn't so much as flinch.

"Boop," said Jack.

And Seleucia Deacon, Grandmaster of the Worshipful Company

of Whatevers, second in Precedence among the Chapmen's Guilds, and partner to the Great Merchant Morvengarde, disintegrated.

This was not like the evanescence of Lady Xiaoming, who had unbodied in a swirling rain of glowing sparks. No, *this* was like a bit of firewood crumbling clumsily to pieces when every scrap of useful fuel has been burned away. When there is nothing left but husk, and nothing to hold the husk together. She was there, and then she was gone, leaving only soot to settle into the grain of the old boards of the pier.

Jack Hellcoal shook his hand again and closed his lantern. "Make it right," he said evenly. Then he stepped lightly off the pier onto the shore, picked up his carpetbag, and walked away into the night, tossing the words "See you both again" over his shoulder and leaving Trigemine and Blister staring, stunned, at the place where Seleucia Deacon had been.

"I guess the stories are true," Trigemine said numbly.

Blister dropped his head into shaking hands. Then he looked up sharply. "Not it."

"What the hell are you talking about?"

"Not it," Blister repeated. "I'm *not* going to be the one to tell Morvengarde about all this. Not it."

Trigemine swore. "The Bluecrownes will answer for this one day," he muttered. "Some time, in some future, those two are going to answer for everything."

FIFTEEN

HOME

FAMILIAR, careful hands took Liao from Lucy's arms, and a moment later she was lying on the deck of the *Left-Handed Fate*'s launch, staring up at the night sky. She felt wrapped in love and the sense of home: the family of seamen who were like a whole crew of uncles and great-uncles and cousins; the launch's familiar creak, like the voice of a sibling; the slide and scrape of the oars in their rowlocks; the predictable shushing lap of water against the bow. Somewhere nearby, her father's arms were waiting.

The boat bumped against the side of the schooner in a manner that would never have been tolerated under normal circumstances, and Lucy was handed up with a tenderness that she ordinarily would not have countenanced. It was Captain Bluecrowne himself who took her, and he hugged her so hard she couldn't draw breath to speak. Then he reached for Liao, and for a long time the three of them held one another, saying nothing, while the children streamed water onto the deck.

Liao's eyes were closed, but tears coursed down his cheeks. He shook with soundless weeping. He had remembered.

"What is it, Liao?" their father asked. "You're safe now."

Liao said nothing, merely shook his head and continued to cry with his eyes shut tight.

"May I tell him, Liao?" Lucy asked softly. Liao gave no answer, only buried his wet face in Captain Bluecrowne's lapel, and Lucy suddenly discovered she didn't know if she could say the words aloud. Grief welled up, filling her so completely that it began to squeeze out the corners of her eyes and spill down her cheeks as well.

Their father hugged Liao closer. "Tell me what?" he asked very gently.

Lucy wiped her face and forced herself to speak. "Jìmǔ." She licked her lips and realized she had no idea how to explain what had happened. There had been strange words and impossible-seeming comparisons to foxes and ships of the line, and then there had been the crane . . . In the end, only one thing seemed at all clear. "I believe she is gone, Papa."

Captain Bluecrowne blinked. "Gone?" The color drained from his face. "What do you mean, gone?"

"I —" Lucy looked helplessly at her even more helpless brother. "I don't know, Papa. I don't know what happened. She was hit with a ball of fire and she . . . she disappeared. She went to pieces. But," she added quickly, "not as if . . . not . . ."

Liao mumbled something against their father's coat. "Say that again, Liao," Captain Bluecrowne said.

"*Shījiě*," came the small, muffled voice. "She has been unbodied."

"Unbodied? What does that mean? Does it mean . . ." She couldn't quite bring herself to say the word *dead*.

"It has to do with the Way," Liao answered unhappily. "I don't know how to explain in English."

All the muscles in Captain Bluecrowne's face seemed to harden. "I do not pretend to have understood everything Xiaoming told me about . . . about her past and her capabilities. But she did speak about something she called the Way."

"What are you talking about?" Lucy asked numbly. "You never told me any of this." She wasn't sure what *this* was, but clearly Liao and her father knew.

"I thought it was best if Xiaoming explained it to you when she chose to share it. Because I didn't understand it." He blinked hard. "And because, I suppose, I didn't completely believe it. Liao." He pulled the boy away from him very gently and peered into his face. Her father hesitated in exactly the same way Liao did when he was trying to articulate something he found confusing. "How much of it is true?" he asked at last.

Liao seemed to understand perfectly what their father was asking. "It *is* true, Papa. All of it. Mama is a *fāngshì*. And, which is more, she is a *xiān*. A . . . celestial being," he added slowly, choosing his words carefully. "But she is gone to us. For now." His voice was small and sad.

Lucy waited, uncomprehending, for Liao to explain. How could one be gone "for now"?

But if Captain Bluecrowne was confused by this, he didn't show it. "For how long?" he asked. Liao raised his shoulders. "My lifetime? Yours?" He got the word *yours* out with difficulty.

"I don't know," Liao whispered. "I don't know." And he put his hands over his face and dropped to his knees and that terrible silent lamentation began to shake his little body again.

Lucy put her arms around him and looked up at her father. "I don't understand, Papa."

"No more do I," Captain Bluecrowne admitted. He seemed older, suddenly, and utterly heartbroken.

And that was when Lucy remembered that she had loved Xiaoming too. The ache rose like gorge again, and she nearly choked on the first sob that tore itself from her.

Liao and Xiaoming had been a distant family for half her life, but they were her family as much as the crew of the *Fate*. As much as her own mother had been her family.

The only thing that had made the idea of living ashore at all bearable was the promise that Lucy and Liao and Xiaoming would be with one another, and that sometimes her father would be there too, and they would all be a family together.

But not anymore.

◈

The next morning, Lucy awoke in her beloved cubbyhole of a cabin to the sound of the bells that had marked the hours for her entire life. She had dreamed of cranes and exploding rockets and the cutter that had been her first command for so brief a time. Sadness for Xiaoming and for the *Driven Star* battled with the joy of waking aboard the *Left-Handed Fate*. Then, out of the extraordinary blend of emotions, a single thought rose: *What happens now?*

Garvett's brisk knock sounded on her door. He peeked in, and the smell of strong coffee sidled past him and into the cabin. "Begging your pardon, miss, but the captain's compliments, and would you like to take breakfast with him or should you like to sleep on a bit?"

Lucy was out of her hammock in a flash. "With him, if you please, Garvett."

The steward touched his knuckle to his temple, then hesitated before speaking again. "We was making this for you, miss, Kendrick and me. He did the sewing and I did the embroidery. Don't know but that you might not want it now." He held out a handful of canvas. "New ditty bag, you see."

Lucy smoothed out the cloth. There was the house at the top of the hill, picked out in Garvett's precise embroidery. There were the bell tower from Riga, the roof tiles from China, the bow windows from Malta, and the stained-glass windows from the family house in England. On the carefully stitched door he'd even added the symbols that Liao had decided spelled *Bluecrowne* in Chinese. Lucy touched them with a shaking finger.

"Got those from this," Garvett added, holding out a parcel the size of her palm. "Which the armorer gave me to give to you, if you still want it."

Lucy took the package and tucked it into the embroidered bag. "Thank you, Garvett," she said solemnly. "Yes, please. I should like to keep them both."

When she arrived at the door of her father's cabin, it was Liao who opened it. Their father was not within, but Lucy could see the makeshift bunk where Liao had slept, not wanting to be separated from his only remaining parent.

She hugged him close. "How do you do today, Liao?"

"I hope we shall have ship's biscuit" was all he said.

Captain Bluecrowne spoke from behind Lucy. "Ship's biscuit aplenty. Garvett's even roused out some of the crunchy sort you like best. But Lucy shall have to make do with soft-tack, toasted up," he added with a tired attempt at a smile.

"Don't be silly," Liao said indignantly. "I'll share mine with Lucy, even if there's only a little bit."

Lucy patted his shoulder. "That's all right, Liao. I like the soft kind best at any rate, even if it hasn't got any weevils to knock out of it."

Liao shook his head incredulously.

The three of them took their meal in the captain's cabin, seated around his desk as had long been their custom. As they ate, Lucy learned from her father that a party from the *Fate* had gone to the house where the peddlers had taken Liao, but had found it looking as though no one had lived there for some time. There had been no broken stringed instrument, no carved candlestick, and no silver wire that might have held down a black and white and red crane. No sorcerous peddlers, certainly—only charred ground and the scent of spent powder to mark that any-one had been there at all.

At last, when their meal was finished, Captain Bluecrowne set down his coffee cup. "Kendrick will have your dunnage aboard by noon," he said. "We shall stop in Flotilla to finish the coppering, and then we shall be done with Nagspeake for now."

"Our dunnage?" Lucy's heart leapt. "Liao and I are to go with you?"

"Yes." There were lines on his face that Lucy was certain had not been there before. "I don't know yet what I shall do about the property here, but I cannot see any other option but that you two come away with us again. I suppose I could leave Kendrick and Garvett to keep house for you, but that isn't the arrangement I wanted." He smiled sadly at Liao. "I had imagined my family safe at home, yes, but in those imaginings, when I left you to go back to sea, I was always leaving you with Xiaoming. I never imagined leaving you behind with no parent at all." Captain Bluecrowne thumped his desk with one palm. "So I'm afraid it's back to sea with you both."

Lucy caught her breath, hardly daring to believe what she'd just heard. "We . . . we may ship with you again?"

"Yes, my love." He smiled, and Lucy could tell he was trying to make it a cheerful smile, but there was deep regret behind it. "We shall simply have to go on wishing confusion to Bonaparte, and hope that somehow England may keep peace with the Americans."

"All right," Liao said quietly.

Lucy nodded, unable to decide whether it was unbecoming, under the circumstances, to feel as relieved, as joyful, as this news made her. To go back to sea had been her only wish, but she was getting that wish only because Xiaoming was gone. And Liao—her brother seemed so lost and small that the lion's share of her happiness dissolved.

"May we go back once more?" she asked. "Liao and I?"

"Why?" Liao asked.

"Because, Liao. Please, Papa?"

"If you like," her father said. "You may have my gig and Kendrick when he returns."

The coxswain was back well before noon. It didn't take long to ship the belongings of two children who, up until now, had been living in cabins the size of closets. By one o'clock, Lucy and Liao were climbing the endless stairs up the cliff with Kendrick on their heels.

They paused now and then to rest, and each time, Lucy looked down at the river below, hardly daring to believe her next trip upon it would take her back to the *Fate* for good. Hardly daring to believe the schooner was to be her home once more. And yet she tried to focus on that, tried even though it felt wrong to do it, beacuse otherwise all she could think was *Jĭmŭ, Jĭmŭ, Jĭmŭ.*

They reached the house at last, and Lucy felt a sharp pang of tenderness for her father, who had caused this bizarre place to be built out of so many of her fondest shore-going memories. *It really is a splendid place,* she thought miserably. *I should have loved it straight away.*

"I'll wait here, shall I, miss?" Kendrick asked quietly from the top of the stairs.

Lucy nodded, and she and Liao walked together across the

lawn. As they went, Liao looked at the remains of his workshop, still scattered across the grass. "What have we come back for, Lucy?" he asked, his voice terribly small.

She took the new ditty bag from around her neck and showed him the symbols stitched on the door. "Are these rendered aright?"

He brightened. "Yes. Perfectly."

"Good." She reached inside and took out the armorer's package. "Here."

Liao undid the wrapping and touched the key and fob that lay nestled in the paper. On the fob, inside a hammered circle of iron, was a small five-pointed crown enameled with blue.

"Turn it over," Lucy said. Her brother obeyed and gazed down at those same symbols cut neatly into the fob's other side. "It was meant to be a gift for Jìmǔ," Lucy told him quietly.

Liao gave a single, shaky sniffle. He took Lucy's hand and together they walked up the stairs and onto the porch.

She waited as he opened the door for one last look inside, closed it again, put the key in the lock, and turned it. Then Liao folded the key and fob inside their wrappings and slid the parcel under the door.

"So she will have it when she comes home," he said solemnly.

Lucy nodded, blinking hard. She took her brother's hand again, and the two of them walked down the stairs and back toward the sea once more.

AUTHOR'S NOTE

Much of the research for what would become *Bluecrowne* began seven or eight years ago during the writing of *The Broken Lands,* long before I had any idea of this particular book. A lot of the later research was dual-purposed; at the time I was working on *Bluecrowne* I was also writing *The Left-Handed Fate,* Lucy and Liao's later adventures during the early months of the War of 1812. A complete bibliography of the sources I used would take pages, but for those who are interested in alchemy, fireworks, the Napoleonic Wars, or navigational trigonometry, here's a small assortment of the books I think were most important to me during the writing of *Bluecrowne.*

Both Lucy Bluecrowne and Foulk Trigemine would recommend reading about trigonometry for their respective types of navigation; I read *Heavenly Mathematics: The Forgotten Art of Spherical Trigonometry* by Glen Van Brummelen. I devoured Patrick O'Brian's Aubrey/Maturin books; they're fiction, but they are so rich with detail about life aboard ships of war in the late eighteenth and early nineteenth centuries that they were invaluable. Dean King's companion and lexicon, *A Sea of Words,* was never far from my elbow. (Also, for a wonderful leap into shipboard life, why not start your reading with Lucy Bellwood's excellent *Baggywrinkles: A Lubber's Guide to Life at Sea?*)

For Xiaoming's arts of *wàidān,* I began with Fabrizio Pregadio's *Great Clarity: Daoism and Alchemy in Early Medieval China; A Study of Chinese Alchemy* by Obed Simon Johnson; and *Sources of Shang History: The Oracle-Bone Inscriptions of Bronze Age China* by David N. Keightley. These were the sources of the translations I used for specific alchemical terms and components, as well as most of the details of the scapular divination and the possibility that the Emperor Shun had a daughter called Xiaoming. But as ever, responsibility for any errors or acts of excessive whimsy is mine alone.

Liao and his fireworks owe much to these same books, as well as Jack Kelly's *Gunpowder: Alchemy, Bombards, & Pyrotechnics: The History of the Explosive that Changed the World;* Simon Werrett's *Fireworks: Pyrotechnic Arts & Sciences in European History; The Complete Art of Firework-Making* by Thomas Kentish; *The Pyrotechnist's Companion: Or, a Familiar System of Recreative Fireworks* by G. W. Mortimer; and *Chemistry and the Making of Fireworks* (Anonymous).

Oh, and it's no secret that my books so far all share a world. If you enjoyed *Bluecrowne* and would like to know more about the characters you've met in these pages, here's where to go to find them again. Find Lucy and Liao and the crew of the *Fate* in *The Left-Handed Fate;* find Liao and his pyrotechnics in *The Broken*

Lands; find the Jumper and the Ironmonger in *The Boneshaker* and *The Kairos Mechanism* (where you will also meet Trigemine once more); find the house on the hill (and a few things that were left behind in it) in *Greenglass House* and *Ghosts of Greenglass House.*

ACKNOWLEDGMENTS

This book began its life as part of a series of short novels I called my Arcana Project, which I self-published using Kickstarter and the Espresso Book Machine that used to live at my beloved McNally Jackson. I never did much to publicize the Arcana books; I hoped those who loved my other stories would sort of happen across them almost by accident and feel like they'd found a surprise hidden especially for intrepid readers to find. *Bluecrowne* was originally published in 2014 alongside *Greenglass House;* the idea was to tell the story of why the family who built the house never lived in it. It was the second Arcana book, following *The Kairos Mechanism,* but in the world of the books, *Bluecrowne* happens first, so it's fitting that it gets to be the first one given new life in this beautiful hardcover.

There are two sets of people I owe great thanks to for the book you're now reading.

If not for the Kickstarter backers of the original version, the friends who helped create a bunch of wonderful rewards for those backers, and the bloggers who helped to spread the word about the campaign, *Bluecrowne* would probably never have been completed. The first draft wasn't finished by the time I had my son, so if I hadn't clearly owed a book to the people who'd believed in that book enough to put money into it, I might never have gotten the thing done. (And without my dear friends Julie Hibshoosh and Ray Rupelli, who took baby detail over and over, I still might not have pulled it off.) Emma Humphrey, Dhonielle Clayton, Mike Lewis, Cynthia Kennedy Henzel, Heidi Ayarbe, and Cathy Giordano read early drafts and gave me much-needed feedback. David Antscherl made sure I didn't make any glaring nautical mistakes. Andrea Offermann created the original artwork a cut paper silhouette cover and a matching vignette—and recruited designer Miwako Feuer, who (among other things) created a custom, ironwork-inspired font for the title. Beth Steidle and Raffe Jefferson at McNally Jackson made sure we had our formatting and colors right so that the final book came off the Espresso Book Machine looking like a little gem. Thirteen young artists created art for the illustrated edition of that first version, for which Kat Yeh and Cindy Pon gave me some important feedback. My brother, Bud Chell, did significant troubleshooting more than once to cover my lack of technical prowess. I am so grateful to every one of you. Thank you.

Being offered the chance to revisit *Bluecrowne* was a totally unexpected gift, and the first thanks must, as ever, go to my brilliant editor, Lynne Polvino, for taking a chance on it, for whipping it into shape, and for assembling a dream team to bring this new version into being: Jaime Zollars, who always brings Nagspeake to life so beautifully, created the new cover; the gorgeous interior illustrations were done by Nicole Wong, and I'm not totally convinced she can't somehow see directly into my imagination; and finally, Sharismar Rodriguez, who has designed almost all my books, brought it all together. Thank you all for making this book look so beautiful. This version also owes a great debt to Karen Bao and Judy Lin, both of whom helped me make the Bluecrowne family and their story richer. Thank you both so much. Caryn Schwartz was kind enough to render some additional assistance with the tone marks, especially on some of the more obscure chemical terms. And to my wonderful agent, Barry Goldblatt, who has done so much to change the course of my career: I couldn't have done this without you.

Finally, the adventures of Lucy, Liao, and the crew of the *Left-Handed Fate* began when my husband, Nathan, twisted my arm mercilessly until I began reading Patrick O'Brian. My life is better for having read the adventures of Jack Aubrey and Stephen Maturin, and I can't recommend them highly enough—they're funny and boisterous and heartbreaking and truly thumping great tales. Sometime during my second reading of the series, Nathan suggested that a ship of war during this era would be a brilliant setting for a middle grade novel, and he was right. Both *Bluecrowne* and *The Left-Handed Fate* owe quite a lot to Nathan and Patrick O'Brian, but they also owe a great deal to my father and my grandfather, both of whom served in the US Navy and later gave me a love of the water and of things that sail upon it. So last of all, thanks to Dad and Granddad, with all my love.